CROSSOVER DRIBBLE

PJ Farris

CROSSOVER DRIBBLE

PJ Farris

All Rights Reserved

Mayhaven Publishing, Inc.
PO Box 557
Mahomet, IL 61853

Cover Art and Design: Jack Davis

Copyright © 2007 P. J. Farris
First Edition—First Printing 2007
ISBN 13: 978-193227843-9
ISBN 10: 193227843-5
Library of Congress Cataloging Number: 2007935486
Printed in USA

Dedicated to my father and my son,
and to all devoted basketball players and fans.

PJ Farris

Chapter 1
Swish

Swish! The ball bounced twice before the boy grabbed it. Squaring his shoulders to the hoop, he released it at the very pinnacle of his jump. Swish!

Dandelion seeds floated in the air and fell upon Scottie, the Border Collie. Curled in a C shape, his eyes never left Joe. He knew that after this daily ritual, another evening's chores would begin.

The ball arched high into the air. Swish!

Dribbling and shooting, Joe moved around the gravel court clicking off the basics in his mind—shoulders square to the basket, weight on the balls of the feet, legs under control. Just as he went up for another jumper, the screen door on the white frame farmhouse slammed. "That kills that," Joe mumbled under his breath as he retrieved the ball.

Fingering a toothpick, Joe's father swiftly booted two calico cats off the door stoop. Startled, the felines leaped for the safety of the flowerbed, landing amidst a yellow and orange splotch of marigolds.

Inhaling a deep breath, Joe spun the brown sphere behind his back. A redwing blackbird issued a scolding cry as it abandoned its fence post perch. *Even the birds know when to vacate the area*, Joe thought as he caught a piercing look from his dad.

"I'll be back in an hour. Gotta get some spark plugs for the tractor," Joe's dad yelled. "Don't overlook your chores."

Joe nodded. His eyes followed the red Ford pickup until it disappeared down the lane in a thick cloud of dust. Grasping the tail of his T-shirt, Joe bent over and used it to wipe away the sweat beads on his face. Picking up the ball, he heaved a thirty-five footer that hit the backboard before ricocheting back at him.

"Brick!" Joe muttered to himself. Shaking his head, he reminded himself of Coach's three rules of being a good player. Fundamentals. Timing. Effort.

Retrieving the rebound, Joe began dribbling. The ball flashed between his legs in a rhythmic fashion, again and again. Next, he positioned his body to protect the ball from an invisible opponent. With a sudden spurt, Joe drove to the basket and laid up a finger roll. Spiraling 'round and 'round and 'round the rim, the ball finally fell through.

Eyes focused and unblinking, Joe concentrated on the basket. The slight breeze felt good as tiny streams of sweat

Crossover Dribble

trickled down his arms.

Okay, Joe thought. *Put it all together. Concentrate. Do the ritual. Toe the line with my right foot. Keep my feet shoulder width apart, left foot slightly behind the line. Lock my eyes on the basket. Dribble twice. Put the ball on my right fingertips and use my left hand to guide it. Shoot.*

The shot banked off the backboard, hitting the lip of the rim and bounced off.

"Aaauuggh!" Joe moaned as he reached into his back pocket and extracted a laminated index card.

BEEF Your Shots

B—Balance: Keep feet together, shoulder-width apart. Shooting foot should be slightly in front of your non-shooting foot. Align your body at a square to the basket.

E—Eyes: Choose a target (the front of the rim, the center of the hoop) and focus on that through your shot.

E—Elbow: Cock your elbow to a 90 degree angle. There should be wrinkles on the back of your wrist. Rest the ball on the pads of your fingers with the center of the ball on your index finger. Put your guide hand on the side of the ball, not under it.

F—Follow Through: Straighten your elbow and release the ball by flicking your wrist. Pretend you're reaching into the hoop when you release the ball. Keep the guide hand straight and don't use it to push the ball.

NOTE: Jump Shot: For distance, add a jump. Don't push

the ball with your arms. All the power should come from your legs.

"Okay, let's get it right. Balance, Eyes, Elbow, Follow Through," Joe ticked off the BEEF formula. Bending his knees slightly and keeping his right elbow close to his body, Joe stared at the rim. With his fingertips, he shot, careful to follow through with his wrist and hand, moving as though he was reaching into a cookie jar on the top shelf in the kitchen. The ball spun in the air toward the basket and went through the hoop. Joe watched the net dance.

Sweet, Joe thought, *ninety-nine more to go.*

Joe toed the line, located the goal, and dribbled twice. *BEEF,* he thought as he sent his shot skyward toward the iron, waving it good bye with his fingers. *Swish!* Again he retrieved the ball and clicked off the BEEF formula with the same results. His face beamed, *I'm in a zone!*

Retrieving the ball, he repeated the steps like a machine. Again and again the net danced as the ball shot through it.

Just three days earlier, Joe had been in school. Already he missed the pick-up games with the guys during lunch hour. He knew most of his friends were busy working on their game, but unlike him, most lived in town or close to other teammates. Living out in the countryside meant practicing alone, but come camp time, Joe felt he'd be ready to show off his skills with the best of the campers.

The screen door slammed again. His mother announced

Crossover Dribble

from the porch, "Time to do your chores, Joe. I'll start supper."

"Sure thing, Mom." In one motion, Joe deftly rolled the basketball into the garage and grabbed a bucket. Sensing what was to come, Scottie raced Joe to the henhouse.

Taking a deep breath and holding it, Joe unlatched the door. Quickly his lungs filled with the horrendous smell of the droppings. Even the eager stock dog kept his distance.

"If I could figure out a way to stay outside and still gather the eggs, I'd do it, Scottie," Joe muttered. Each breath was held as long as possible before inhaling another odoriferous whiff of air. "Yuck! And next week I'll have to clean out this mess."

Silently, Joe slid through the doorway.

"Easy there. Okay ladies, don't get your feathers ruffled. It's just me—Joe, the egg man. I'll be outta here in no time." A white hen flew up, hitting him in the shoulder. Startled, he stepped back as the other chickens began clucking and squawking. Dust and feathers filled the air, causing Joe to cough. "Augh! What the heck's the matter with you hens?"

Just then he caught a glimpse of Scottie standing in the doorway. "Doggone it, Scottie, get your nose out of here!" Joe turned and lowered his voice. "Settle down, girls, settle down. Nuthin' to fuss about."

The soft tones of Joe's voice soon soothed the flock. The old bronze rooster with his lopsided red comb tipped his head sideways to watch the intruder. Cautiously, silently, Joe

PJ Farris

removed the eggs from the nests two at a time. As if in slow motion he skillfully slipped his hand in under a red hen seated on a nest. Delicately, Joe pulled out a freshly laid egg, still warm, leaving the hen undisturbed. "seventeen, eighteen," he counted.

Timing is everything, Joe thought, *in basketball and in farming. In a couple of hours one of these hens might have broken an egg by stepping on it. Then Dad would blame me.*

Reaching to fasten the henhouse door, Joe abruptly stopped and listened. The wail of a siren echoed across the countryside. He didn't move until it died away.

Chapter 2
Wonder

Wonder what that's all about, thought Joe as he peered across newly tilled fields. *Probably a deputy caught one of the high school guys speeding.*

After putting the bucket of eggs inside the back door, Joe ambled out to the wooden pasture gate. Scissoring his legs, he crossed over it. Scottie scurried through a nearby hole in the fence. Leaping along, the dog's black and white fur stood out against the vibrant green meadow grass.

Captain, Joe's grandfather, had told him that Border Collies are natural stock dogs. "That dog would bring up the cows four or five times a day if you asked him to. Why, shoot fire! He'd wear the pads off of his feet if it meant herding the cattle or sorting hogs for market," Captain had explained. "Nobody works as hard as that dog."

Dashing here and there, Scottie was checking out new scents. The dog flushed a family of quail hidden in the tall

PJ Farris

grass along the fence row. Bounding over the hillside to where the cattle were grazing, Scottie surveyed the entire herd as he shifted into a graceful trot, circling the animals. Clearly, Scottie relished this daily task.

With Scottie's speed and moves, Joe contemplated, *I'd be some basketball player. Nobody could stop me.* "Yes sir, Scottie, you have the two A's a good player needs—acceleration and agility. Too bad you're so short."

Reaching down for a foxtail weed, Joe started chewing on the stem without sacrificing a stride. A pair of barn swallows swooped low, gracefully gobbling up unsuspecting mosquitoes.

Cowpies randomly dotted the path. Joe began trotting around them, pretending he was making moves on the basketball court. He dashed toward a cowpie and did a 360 spin move before pretending to toss up a shot from the paint.

"Listen up, Scottie. Those two tall cowpies there would be the double stack on the right side of the paint. That little cowpie would be the give and go, and those over there would be the pick and roll." Joe chuckled. *What would Coach think of designing plays using manure piles?*

Amused, Joe remembered plays Coach didn't design—like when Scooter passed the ball between the legs of a lanky opposing center to Kurtis for an uncontested lay up, or when Chase's cousin was playing on the Linton squad and unintentionally tapped a rebound right to Chase, who shot it

Crossover Dribble

with four seconds left—to win the game. Their families didn't talk for weeks. Then at the next game, Mitch took a sign from his dad's construction company and taped it to the back of big Jim Bob's shorts—"Oversized Load" it read. The crowd loved it. Then there was the time the player from Winchester was sent in to sub. When he pulled off his warmups, the fans hooted and made catcalls. The player turned red as a beet when he realized he'd forgotten to put on his shorts and was standing there in his briefs. Thank goodness for long jerseys.

Two cows headed north in the opposite direction from the barnyard bringing Joe back to the job at hand. "Get around 'em Scottie!"

Shooting past Joe, Scottie quickly returned the two cows to the group.

"Good dog!" shouted Joe.

With both ears standing at alert, Scottie crouched low before bolting to the right in a big circle around the herd of cattle. Then he darted off, swinging wide, slowly moving the herd back toward the barnyard. A black cow with a white face stopped to nibble off a clump of grass. Peering at the dog, the cow chewed in a slow, deliberate rhythm as she stood her ground. As Scottie crept up, the old cow defiantly lowered her head. Scottie stared at the cow that stared back, refusing to budge, but when he took a step toward her, she gave up her bluff and trotted off toward the rest of the herd. As she

PJ Farris

approached a small gully, the cow broke into a run and jumped the small stream. Young calves kicked up their heels and began running alongside her.

"Ho! Scottie, ho!" Joe called. Scottie slowed to a trot, trailing the cattle, keeping an alert eye out for stragglers. Joe clucked his tongue. At this signal, Scottie rushed at a pokey cow and nipped at her heel. The cow hightailed it to the herd.

"Atta boy, Scottie!"

As the cattle sauntered into the barnlot, Joe gave Scottie a quick pat on the head. "Feeding time for us, fella."

As Joe walked back to the house, he pulled out a second card with another of Coach's tips: "If someone steals the ball from you, your first reaction will be anger and frustration. You'll want to get even and try to steal the ball back. This almost always ends up in a foul being called on you. Instead of trying to get even, keep your composure. Maintain your poise—and use your head. Remember, it's a long game."

Stay calm, Joe thought. *Yeah, Coach, sure. Easier said than done. Like last February's game with Central, a real tough team that played every game down to the wire. That puny little seventh-grade guard reached out and tapped the ball away from me. The guy took off like someone was chasing him with a cattle prod. By the time I caught up, I could only slap the guard's arm as he went in for the lay up. The shot went in. Then the guy sank the free throw. Final score: Central 47—Cedarsburg 46. I vomited in the locker room—*

Crossover Dribble

a taste that lingered in my mouth for days.

"Yeah, Coach, don't worry. I've learned to keep my cool under pressure," Joe muttered. Scottie pricked his ears and cocked his head. "Okay, Scottie, so I don't always stay calm But some day they're goin' to call me Ice Man 'cause I won't let anything make me lose my cool."

When Joe entered the big farm kitchen, his mom was stirring limp spaghetti into an iron skillet of tomato sauce and hamburger. The spices tantalized his nostrils.

"Smells good!" Joe noted, pouring himself a tumbler of milk.

"Guess your dad got tied up," his mom said as she put bread and butter on the table. "Let's go ahead and eat. When his stomach starts growling, he'll head for home lickety split."

"Great, I'm starving."

Salad wasn't his favorite, but Joe snarfed it down along with two plates of pasta. A gargantuan piece of cherry cobbler topped off the meal.

"Had enough? Or should I butcher a hog to tide you over?" joked his mom.

Joe blushed as she began clearing the table.

"Joe, get yesterday's newspaper and cover the leftovers on the table. Don't use the page with the death announcements, though."

"Sure, Mom, but why are you so superstitious? It's not like they're going to know about it."

PJ Farris

"Superstitious, am I?" she countered. "And who wore the same pair of socks to every basketball game last season?" She paused. "You'd better water the livestock just in case Dad doesn't come back soon. And if he thinks you've been playing basketball, he'll be fit to be tied."

"Yeah, I know." *Dad blew up when I asked to go to basketball camp in the first place,* Joe thought, *insisting I pay for it. He wasn't going to let me go except you and Captain spoke up for me. Took him three weeks to give me the go ahead. Ever since, he's complained to no end about having to do my chores for me while I'm gone.*

The phone rang. Joe answered, "Hello."

A woman's voice asked, "May I speak to Mrs. Perkins?"

"Sure." Joe handed the phone to his mom. "It's for you."

His mom wiped her hands on a towel and reached for the receiver. "Hello, this is Mrs. Perkins."

Joe noticed his mom suddenly stiffen.

"What happened?" she asked, her usual breezy tone now somber. "Yes, of course. His leg, too?" She turned and looked at Joe. "I'm on my way right now."

She hung up the phone, but her thin fingers remained on the receiver. For Joe, the moment of stillness was eerie.

Slowly she turned toward him. "Your dad's been in a bad accident."

"What happened?"

"He was in a wreck over by Jeffer's corner. They're

18

Crossover Dribble

going to have to operate on him to stop the internal bleeding." Her face was blank.

Stunned, Joe's heartbeat quickened. Then he remembered the siren. Probably the sheriff or the ambulance, and it was for his dad.

"Pretty bad, huh?" Joe asked softly.

"It's not good, Joe. The woman said his leg is pretty messed up, too."

Joe asked, "Which one?"

His mom tilted her head as she faced her son, saying softly, "Oh, Joe, I didn't even think to ask."

"Well, what happened?"

Reaching into the closet for her sweater, she said, "A car ran the stop sign and plowed right into him."

"Whew! Who did it?"

"They didn't say. I just know your dad needs me."

Joe nodded.

"You stay here and finish the chores." She picked up her purse and car keys off of the kitchen counter. "And don't forget to check on Sarsaparilla. Dad's been worried about her."

Silently Joe shook his head, plunging his hands deep into the pockets of his jeans.

"I'll call you from the hospital as soon as I find anything out." As she reached for the door handle, his mom stopped and tugged on his baseball cap. "Don't worry, Joe. He'll be fine," she said.

PJ Farris

Joe noticed, though, that her face was filled with worry. Her words echoed through his head like a giant pinball.

Once again Joe watched dust swirl down the lane, this time engulfing their old brown sedan.

Maybe I should've gone with her, he thought. *But she said everything will be fine.* Deep inside Joe's fears festered.

"It can't be that bad. Nothing can ever be that bad." Joe's voice was barely an undertone. Clenching his right hand into a fist, he slammed it hard into his left palm.

His heart ached and he had difficulty breathing, as if a vise had tightened and encircled his chest. A chill ran through him and he shuddered. "Come on, pull it together. Focus on the chores. Concentrate." He couldn't resist keeping the car in sight until it disappeared behind the neighbor's huge white dairy barn.

Scottie followed quietly in Joe's footsteps to the farrowing shed. The dozing sows were startled by Joe and Scottie's unexpected appearance and they promptly began a chorus of loud grunts. Squeals of the little baby pigs soon joined in as they scrambled awake.

"Well, Scottie, how much feed do you think a sow can eat? I have no idea. Geez, I don't even know how much to feed the cows or the calves, and I'll bet I've seen Dad do it a thousand times." Perplexed, he shrugged and gave Scottie a quick pat before filling a bucket with feed.

Impatiently, Scottie began pacing back and forth, look-

Crossover Dribble

ing at his master. Joe sighed and grabbed the feed wagon.

"Each of you mamas gets a scoop of feed and a trough of water. No complaints, you hear me?" Joe moved along from pen to pen. "I'm just the sub. The starter will be back before you know it." *At least I hope so*, he thought. *If not, I can kiss basketball camp good-bye.* Joe kicked a clump of sawdust shavings, spraying wooden sprinkles across the floor.

A young pig ran past Joe. "Go get that pig!" Dutifully, Scottie began the chase. Squealing, the pig raced down the runway.

"Atta boy, Scottie, you corner him and I'll catch him." Scottie herded the pig back toward the pen. Joe lunged, missing him by inches. The dog stopped and stared at Joe.

"I blew it, fella. That pig is fast! Run him past me again, Scottie. I'll catch him this time. Guaranteed!"

Again Scottie turned the pig around. This time, as it tried to dart by, Joe grabbed it.

"Scottie," Joe grimaced, "you didn't have to run him through the crap!" Joe's white T-shirt was smeared with brown spots and so was Scottie's head.

"So, little guy," Joe looked the baby pig in the eye, "you didn't like being on your own as much as you thought you would, huh? Bet Mama looks pretty good to you now." The pig grunted as Joe put it back in its pen.

"Go tell your brothers and sisters about your big adventure. Also be sure to tell them life's better *inside* the pen than

PJ Farris

out 'cause I don't have time to chase pigs."

After rinsing off his hands at a spigot, Joe went to the hog lot. "We'd better check the hog feeders, Scottie."

As Joe attempted to swing up to grab the top of the feeder bin, he slipped and scratched his hand. Dangling from one arm, he secured his right foot on a brace. Scottie looked at him, ears alert.

Joe peered inside the clogged feeder. "Dang it! Last night's rain leaked into the bin." He stretched his slender body to grab the chunks of caked feed, tossing them into an empty bucket on the ground.

"Done!" Joe drew back as he shut the feeder lid. Jumping down, he said, "The hogs have dry feed now so they'll fill their tummies up and sleep well tonight."

Next Joe went to check on Sassy. Sarsaparilla was his dad's favorite cow. The family figured Joe's nickname of Sassy was short for Sarsaparilla, but Joe called her Sassy because she was nothing short of being a big pain in the neck for him. Her mom didn't claim her when she was born, so Sassy had to be bottle-fed by Joe before he went to school each morning, and each evening when he got home. Now full grown, she was like a 1300 pound puppy that would, if you weren't careful, run you over whenever she pleased. Any day now she'd deliver her first calf.

"There you are, you big beautiful bovine," Joe said as he poured the mixture of ground corn and molasses into a rub-

Crossover Dribble

ber tub. "You look okay to me, but then, what do I know?" Filling her mouth with the sugar sweet feed, Sassy turned to gaze at Joe.

"Saw, girl, saw," Joe patted Sassy's side to keep her calm. Shifting her weight from one hind foot to the other, Sassy swatted her long black tail at a large horsefly nibbling on her back.

Scottie meandered over towards them. Sassy snorted and stomped her foot at the dog. Quickly the cow swung around. Joe urged, "Saw, Sassy, saw now," as he tried to back out of the way. But he moved too slowly. Sassy's head smacked him hard in the forehead. With a loud thud, Joe fell to the ground.

Chapter 3
Reality

A sound like water running and the smell of ammonia awakened Joe as hot yellow liquid splashed on his leg.

"Get outta here, you stupid cow!" Joe shouted as he struggled to sit up. "First you try to decapitate me, then you try to drown me by peeing on me. Sassy, I swear you're as evil as Satan himself!"

Scottie ambled over to his master. Despite the wet, warm jeans, Joe shivered. As he reached to put his arms around the dog, Scottie's tongue brushed across Joe's face like sandpaper. "Scottie, your breath is bad news." Joe pushed the dog away. Gingerly, he felt his forehead and inspected his fingertips. "No blood," he whispered as he ruffled the dog's fur, "but it sure hurts like the devil."

Woozy, Joe's head felt like a thunderstorm was going on inside. Out of the corner of his eye, he caught a glimpse of Sassy striding over to graze in his mom's flower garden. She

Crossover Dribble

stopped to feed on the red petunias.

"Cripes!" Joe picked up his baseball cap and slammed it into the dirt. "Scottie! Come on fella! Go get Sassy!" The black and white dog scampered through the gate, circled around the cow, and crouched low. The cow's head hovered over the dog for a moment before Sassy trotted back into the pen.

"That'll do Scottie," Joe said as he pulled himself up on the fence.

I should've fastened the gate when I came in, he thought as he put the cow into the pen. *Dad will holler at me for letting her get out. If she's trampled Mom's flowers, he'll be twice as mad.*

After a quick check of the slightly battered petunias, Joe and Scottie headed across the barnyard to the house.

By the time Joe peered into the bathroom mirror, the lump on his head was the size of a silver dollar. Wincing, he mumbled, "That old heifer never did like me. Shouldn't be surprised that she tried to kill me."

After showering, Joe went downstairs, carefully taking each step along the way. As he grabbed an ice bag from the freezer for his head, the grandfather clock in the hallway began to strike. Bong! Bong! Bong! It was as if his head was being pounded by a relentless drummer.

"Nine o'clock! It took me over three hours to do the chores! Three hours! I hate farming! I hate it!" He threw himself down on the couch and stared at the slowly revolv-

PJ Farris

ing ceiling fan above him.

When he glanced at the answering machine, Joe noticed it had been turned off. A ringing phone was always a nuisance to Joe's dad who lacked the patience to listen to messages people left. "Darn waste of time," he'd protest as he replayed messages left by telemarketers.

Melting ice water ran down Joe's cheek as he stretched out on the couch. *What do I do now*, he thought as he flicked on the TV and surfed the channels. *I could call the hospital, but I didn't even ask which hospital. Smart move. Maybe Captain's heard something.*

Joe's fingers danced across the numbers.

After four long rings, his grandfather answered. "Hello."

"Grandpa, it's me, Joe. Did Mom call you?"

"Yeah, I tried getting you but you didn't answer. I was just heading out the door to to see what happened to you."

Joe took a deep breath and asked, "How's Dad doing?"

"He's out of surgery and in recovery. Guess he's bruised up pretty bad." Joe felt his stomach tighten at his grandfather's words.

Joe asked, "What happened?"

"Some guy ran the stop sign and Mack slammed right into him. Mack's got a long haul before he can back to work." There was a pause on the other end of the line.

Joe felt sick to his stomach.

Finally, Captain spoke. "It could've been a whole lot

Crossover Dribble

worse, Joe." His grandfather's voice faded away.

Joe didn't know what else to say. "Well, I'm fine, Grandpa. I'd better let you go to bed."

"You too, Joe. You must be tired out. Did you get all the chores done? You didn't forget to feed Sassy, did you?"

Why is it that all everyone thinks about is that dumb cow? Joe thought as he gritted his teeth. "Yeah, they're all tucked in. Sassy put up a fuss, but I sang her to sleep with a lullaby."

"That'll be the day," his grandfather chuckled. Joe relaxed a little at the reassuring sound of laughter. "I'll see you in the morning, Joe. Night."

"Night, Captain."

Joe eased himself back on the couch. *Now what,* he thought. *I know. I'll follow coach's advice. Stay calm. Keep poised. Use my head.*

"Good advice, Coach," he said softly as he stood up and made his way to his bedroom. "Besides, I can't do anything to help Dad right now. I'll keep calm and just wait it out."

Wrapping his arm around his pillow, he stared out the window at the moon. Sleep didn't come easy. For hours he tossed and turned. Suddenly he woke, his heart beating rapidly and his hands clammy.

Chapter 4
Voices

Voices in the kitchen startled Joe. His head ached.

"Stayed up late watching TV, did ya, Slats?"

"Slats" was the nickname Joe's grandfather had given him because he was tall and lanky. To tease his grandfather back, Joe called him, "Captain." It was a reminder of a time long ago when, at only 5 feet 10 inches, his grandfather had played center on his high school basketball team and was the team's captain.

"Say, how'd you get that lump on your head?"

"Sassy tried to knock my blooming head off but I'll be okay." Joe flinched as his grandfather touched the bump.

"How's Dad?"

Joe's mother stood beside the stove. "He's pretty banged up," she said. "Good thing he had his seat belt on. Probably saved his life." His mom seemed weary.

Pouring a large glass of orange juice, Joe gulped most of

Crossover Dribble

it down in one swig.

Captain looked over his newspaper. "Oh, by the by, you didn't take care of the feeder calves last night."

"I guess I just forgot about them. Sorry." Joe's face reddened as he shot a glance at Captain. "How'd you know?"

"Listen. That feedlot is quite a distance from the house, but the pathetic sound of those calves bawling can't be missed."

"You can feed them after breakfast, Joe." His mother handed him slices of buttered toast.

"Sorry, Mom." Joe reached for some strips of bacon. "Did they tell you how the accident happened?"

"Bill Yeager ran the stop sign as he was heading to work. He died at the scene," his mom said.

Joe looked down at his plate. *I ride the school bus with the three Yeager kids. It's got to be tough on them.*

His mom went on, "Dad broke his wrist and some ribs, and his leg was smashed up something awful. They think the operation took care of the internal bleeding, though."

She handed him a plate of steaming hot scrambled eggs. *A bum leg. Not good,* he thought.

"I still say he's pretty darn lucky to be alive," said Captain. "He could've been there for hours if Sue Mitchell hadn't come along after her shift at the hospital and found them. She covered Mack up so he wouldn't go into shock and called the ambulance. Your dad's a mighty lucky fellow."

PJ Farris

The pain in Joe's head twisted his mind into knots.

Captain cradled his coffee cup between his hands and stared out the window at the newly plowed field.

"Dad's going to be all right ?" Joe asked. His throat felt parched. Accidents out in the country were serious business.

"That's what the doctor says. He's gone through a lot but he's stable now." She nibbled at a piece of toast, then looked at her son. "We'd better take care of that big lump. Let me look at it." She leaned over Joe's head. "Sassy nailed you a good one."

"I told you it's nothing. Sassy just tattooed me." Joe turned away. "I put ice on it last night." He paused before asking, "When do you think I can see him?"

"I thought I'd catch up on sleep this morning and get some things done around the house." His mother rested her elbows on the table as she ate. "The doctor thought your dad would probably sleep most of the day with all the pain medicine they've given him. We could leave for the hospital about three or so." She refilled the coffee cups.

The Captain pushed his chair away from the table. "We've got plenty to do around here, that's for sure. We can get a lot done before three o'clock. Ain't easy being a farmer, Joe, worse yet being hurt and unable to do anything."

"Mack loves farming," Joe's mom's said, "but it sure brings a lot of stress, having to depend on mother nature's whims. I hope it doesn't rain until the crops are planted.

Crossover Dribble

Then there's all the livestock to take care of. I just don't know..." Her voice trailed away.

Captain interrupted the silence. "The doc'll patch Mack up and he'll be as good as new before you know it." Unexpectedly, Joe felt a spry kick delivered under the table to his outstretched leg. It was followed by Captain's stern look. "We'll manage, right, Slats?"

"Yeah," Joe joined in. "Don't worry, Mom. We can handle the chores and stuff. It'll be okay."

Captain stood up. "What's on the menu, Joe?"

Joe looked up. "Huh?"

"What are we going to do today? You know, what farm work has to get done?"

Stammering, Joe spit out, "I don't know. I guess we'll do the morning feeding." Then he remembered. "I'd better feed the calves first."

"You bet you will. Let's look at your dad's notebook and see what he'd planned for today."

Limping over to the neatly organized roll top desk, Captain pulled a worn spiral notebook off the shelf. "It says here that Mack was planning to plant corn on the Conner place and 20 acres up north."

Joe's mom nodded, "Mack finished disking up there yesterday."

"Well, we'd better get up and at 'em, Slats." Snatching his dirty green cap from the hat rack, Captain went out the

PJ Farris

door with Joe on his heels.

Morning chores went quickly. Sassy seemed content with her breakfast. The feeder calves chomped on their silage. The young pigs squealed as they crowded in for their mother's nipples. With Scottie's help, Joe drove the cattle to the lush green pasture to graze.

Metal lids clanked as the feeder hogs eagerly filled their empty stomachs. Their hunger satisfied, they wandered through the concrete feedlot to a cool, muddy spot where they plopped down to snooze the day away.

"I'll feed the cats and Scottie, then we'll be ready to start planting, Captain." Joe spoke slowly and deliberately to make his voice sound positive—even if he wasn't.

Quietly, Scottie followed Joe to the doghouse. After filling the bowls with food and water, Joe reached for the ring on Scottie's collar. "I know you don't like being chained up all day," he said, "but we can't risk you following the tractor and getting run over by a car." Gently he roughed up the dog's ears. "Don't worry, fella. I'll let you spook a couple of cows this evening and make 'em behave themselves."

Joe walked over to the machinery shed. His dad's rack of tools neatly arranged on pegboard loomed over him. Bins clearly labeled with nuts and bolts of precise sizes rested on a counter. Not a single tool or piece of machinery was out of place. Everything was cleaned, oiled and put away ready for its next use. Folks said you could eat off Joe's mom's floors.

Crossover Dribble

Fact was, the same was true for his dad's shop. Joe gripped the handle of the vise, turning it a revolution without thinking.

"Get a move on, Slats. Hop up in the truck and stack the bags," Captain ordered.

Jumping up on the tailgate, Joe began dragging bags of seed to the front of the truck. After several bags were stacked, his pace noticeably slowed.

"What's the matter?" Captain said.

"These bags are kinda heavy," Joe clenched his teeth as he dragged another bag across the truck bed.

Laughing, Captain said, "These bags ain't heavy at all. They only weigh 40 pounds. When your dad was your size we still used bushel bags—56 pounders they were. After a day of man handling those, you were tuckered out."

Joe thought, *my back will be aching tonight just lugging these 40 pounders.*

"If you weren't so skinny, Slats, you'd be tossin' them like bags of popcorn at the movies!"

"Yeah, sure!" Joe grunted as he shoved a bag with his foot. "I'm not exactly a power forward at 5'11" and 138 pounds."

"Shoot Joe, you're *only* 13. You've got plenty of time to fill out a might."

"Yeah, sure. Take a look at me sideways. People confuse me with an oversized Q-tip." Taking a deep breath, Joe heaved the last seed corn bag on top of the stack in the truck.

PJ Farris

The bag fell back and landed on Joe's knee.

Gritting his teeth, Joe took another grip on the sack. "One, two, three, up you go!" The bag barely made the top of the pile. Joe pushed it up the rest of the way.

"Last bag always is the heaviest, Slats. And for your information, your dad was skinny as a rail at your age. Guess I was, too." Captain slammed the tailgate shut and leaned back on it. "Your mom's plumb tuckered out and worried sick. Go fix some sandwiches for us. And don't forget to bring a jug of ice water. It's goin' to be hotter than a firecracker today."

Finding the refrigerator empty, Joe whipped up four peanut butter and jelly sandwiches. He grabbed some chocolate chip cookies—Captain's favorite—and a couple cans of peaches from the cupboard.

Captain was fidgeting when Joe returned. "I've been thinking, Joe. Do you know how to operate that cotton-pickin' planter?"

Sheepishly, Joe shook his head. "No, I don't."

"Just as I thought. *I* sure don't know anything about it. The thing is too complicated for me—computer counting out the seeds and all. I retired from farming when all this high-tech stuff came along. Let's go take the Ford and the four-row planter. We'll move like a snail but we'll get the job done."

Cinder, Captain's old black and grey dog, greeted them in the driveway of Captain's farmyard. The dog was his

Crossover Dribble

closest companion ever since Joe's grandmother died of cancer two years earlier. Joe patted the friendly dog. "How you doin', girl? Want to ride in the truck today?"

"Naw, Cinder can stay home in the shade. She's been having trouble climbing up in the truck. Guess her arthritis is worse than mine. Right girl?" Slowly, the dog ambled over to the lawn and stretched out in the sunshine.

The old four-row planter had been sitting in the barn where Captain had covered it up with a green tarp years ago.

"Here's the grease gun. You wiggle under there and I'll tell you where to lube 'er up." Joe crawled under the planter and shimmied back and forth as Captain directed, pumping the trigger of the grease gun twice each time.

"Now, let's hitch 'er up and get going," Captain ordered.

Cautiously, Joe backed up the Ford tractor and lowered the hitch. Captain dropped the pins in and stepped away as he hollered, "All set! Follow me!"

The pace Captain set with his pickup was slow and deliberate as he towed the fertilizer wagon behind him. Joe's thoughts rambled as he followed along. *At least I know what I'm doing. This old Ford tractor and I have disked every field Dad's farmed. We might not be as fast as the bigger tractors, but like Captain says, "we'll get the job done."*

A few miles later, a man in a dusty pickup flagged them down. "Too bad about Mack. Must have been a horrible accident," Joe overheard as he climbed down from the tractor.

PJ Farris

"Yeah, too bad about Bill Yeager. Gonna be hard on his wife and kids," Captain said.

"They told me that Yeager just blew right through the stop sign. Mack couldn't help but hit him." Leaning out of the pickup, the farmer spit a long stream of brown tobacco juice onto the pavement.

Captain nodded. "Yeah. Heard they found Yeager's body in a wheat field. If Mack hadn't had his seat belt fastened, he'd have been thrown out and most likely died too."

Joe swallowed hard, his throat parched, wordless. It was just as well because he couldn't think of anything to say.

The farmer adjusted his seed cap and said, "I just came from the Co-op. Old Ben Russell told me he'd take care of spraying nitrogen on the corn for you. He ain't got nothin' to do now that he's retired. Said he'd send you the bill. No charge for the labor. Just give me a jingle if I can do anything. I've got 450 acres of beans to put in, but I'd be glad to help out if I can."

Captain thanked him and Joe waved as the farmer sped off in his pickup.

Turning, Joe stared at Captain, "Nobody told me Dad could've been killed."

"It was an awful wreck, I guess." Captain took his cap off and scratched his head.

Joe raked the toe of his shoe across the pea gravel. "How bad was our truck tore up?"

Crossover Dribble

"He totaled it." Captain pulled out his red handkerchief and blew his nose. "Well, I'm glad Ben'll help us out, but the good Lord helps those who help themselves. Standing around ain't gettin' the corn planted."

Feeling as though his insides were going to explode, Joe made his way back to the tractor. Joe filled his lungs with the clean spring air, hoping his grandfather wasn't looking in the rearview mirror as he wiped tears from his eyes with his shirtsleeve. Putting the tractor into gear, Joe once again took in a deep breath from the fresh morning breeze and followed Captain's pickup down the road.

Chapter 5
Making Sense

Shadows of trees in the fence row loomed like forbidding monsters over the little blue tractor. Captain slowly drove back and forth the length of the long field.

Joe sat on the tailgate watching Captain plant corn. Then he killed some time tossing clods at a nearby fence post. *Well*, he thought, *nothing to do until the seed and fertilizer boxes need refilling. No use wasting my time worrying.*

Reaching into his back pocket, Joe pulled out a plastic bag of Coach's pointers: When you are guarding another player, maintain an athletic stance. Keep your feet shoulder width apart with your weight on the balls of your feet, not your heels. Maintain your balance. Run backwards for half the distance of the court, and then use a cross over step to turn and keep up with the man you're guarding. Practice running backwards so you'll get used to the defensive position.

Makes sense, Joe thought. *Might as well do it.*

Crossover Dribble

Joe practiced running backwards as fast as he could while Captain slowly drove the tractor up and down the long field. The tilled soil made running backwards difficult, causing Joe to fall a few times.

After several attempts at back-pedaling back and forth between the freshly planted rows and the ditch, Joe thought, *No sweat! I'm finally getting the hang of it!*

Suddenly Joe felt his foot slip. "Awwwwww!" he shouted, as he pummeled backwards into the water-filled ditch.

"Yikes!" Mud dripped from his ears as he wiped his hair. Muck and slime oozed from his shirt and pants as he walked back to the pickup. Scrounging behind the seat, he found a dirty pair of Captain's four-buckle overalls and a plaid shirt.

I hope nobody I know drives past, Joe thought as the gap between the too-short pant legs and his muddy sneakers conspicuously revealed his pale white ankles.

Captain stopped for more seed corn. "What in blazes happened to you?" he grinned.

"I fell into the ditch," Joe mumbled.

Holding up Joe's mud-filled jeans, Captain chuckled. "You can plant for awhile since you seem to have a yearning to plant yourself in the dirt!" With that, Captain tossed the jeans in the back of the pickup and lay down across the seat.

Joe had helped his father disk fields lots of times, but he'd never planted before. *Well*, he thought, *it can't be too complicated. Just got to keep the rows straight or Dad will bellyache.*

PJ Farris

Lowering the left row marker, Joe kicked the tractor into gear. He watched as the marker's disk slowly revolved, making a distinct line down the field. A ringneck peasant flew from the underbrush of the fence row, its emerald green neck shimmering in the bright sunlight. Watching the bird fly off, Joe scolded himself for becoming distracted.

Planting isn't so bad, Joe thought. *You just follow the line. If you get off a bit, straighten up the wheels as quick as you can so the whole field won't be crooked. It's as easy as dribbling the ball down a basketball court.*

Joe's mind wandered. *When things get tough, Mom always hangs in there. If the bills seem to come in faster than the money to pay them, she still says we'll be okay. Or if I get a poor grade, she'll tell me to buckle down and spend more time studying, then better grades will come. Even when the team is losing, I hear Mom's voice in the crowd shouting encouragement.*

By lunchtime the field was neatly striped with rows of planted corn. "Let's eat before going to the Conner place. What's for lunch, Cook?" Captain stopped whittling on a stick and peered into the grocery sack and ice chest.

Joe grinned as Captain announced, "Ah, peaches and chocolate chip cookies! My favorites! If I didn't know better I'd think your mom packed the lunch."

Crossover Dribble

Joe was pleased as he wolfed down two sandwiches and four cookies. Captain pulled the lid off his can of peaches and looked again into the paper bag.

"What are you lookin' for?" Joe asked.

"Spoons to eat the peaches with." Captain rattled the sack around.

"Oh, I forgot the spoons," Joe moaned.

"Maybe I can spear them with my pocketknife."

Try as he might, the peaches slipped off Captain's knife and fell into the dirt. "Guess that won't do. Say, I've got a better idea. If we tip the can slightly so the peaches will fall out, we can eat them that way."

Peach syrup trickled down Captain's chin. "Kinda like catching a fish with the side of your mouth. Slippery little things!" Captain remarked as he wiped his chin with his red handkerchief.

Opening his can, Joe tried to follow Captain's advice. But Captain was far nimbler at catching peaches than he was. Joe dropped several, but the few that found their way into his mouth tasted good and the sweet syrup was refreshing.

They loaded the remaining bags of seed corn on top of the planter. Joe headed to the north 20 acres while Captain went back to the farm to get more seed and fertilizer.

By three o'clock, they had finished planting both fields and were back at the farm. Joe parked the Ford tractor and planter under the maple tree. Taking the ice chest and water

PJ Farris

jug out of the pickup, he gave Captain a thumbs-up sign. He unchained Scottie, who raced him to the back door.

"Mom, we're back." Sitting on the back stoop, Joe shook the dirt out of his sneakers. His muddy rolled up jeans and socks looked like giant Tootsie Rolls.

"You've got enough soil there for a vegetable garden," his mother said from behind the screen door. "And what are you doing wearing those overalls?" She laughed. "They look like knickers on you."

With a sheepish grin, Joe said, "I sort of fell in the mud."

"Sort of fell in the mud? I should say so. Now go get cleaned up. Your dad'll be wondering about us."

The hot water from the showerhead pulsated down on Joe's tired muscles. The twisting to watch the planter's marker caused his neck to hurt. His shoulders and back had taken a toll from carrying the heavy bags of seed corn.

Dressed in a pair of clean Levi's, Joe pulled on his cowboy boots. He reached for his basketball jersey since it was so hot, but he changed his mind and settled on wearing a yellow short-sleeved T-shirt.

"Wow! Look at that sunburn!" his mom said. "Why don't you take your shirt off? If we don't take care of that burn, you won't sleep tonight." She went into the kitchen and returned with a cotton ball soaked with vinegar.

Crossover Dribble

The hot sun had forced Joe to peel off his shirt early that morning. Even his stomach was sunburnt. Joe flinched as his mom dabbed the vinegar on his reddened skin.

"This'll take the sting out of it," she said. "Make sure you drink a lot of water, Joe. We don't need you getting dehydrated and having a sunstroke."

When they picked up Captain, he looked fresh and cool in his blue chambray shirt and khaki work pants. The late afternoon sun hit Joe in the eyes, making him realize how tired he was. Leaning his head against the car seat, he dropped off to sleep.

As the car pulled into the hospital parking lot, Joe's mom said, "Wake up. We're here."

"Huh?" Joe stretched and realized where he was.

They followed Joe's mom down one hallway after another, up an elevator, and down a short hallway past a nurses' station to room 237. The strong pungent smell of antiseptic filled the hospital room. Joe looked at the machines and the gauges surrounding his dad's bed. Transparent tubes ran to his dad's nose and hand. A cast was on his left wrist. His broken left leg was stretched out on the bed. The voices from the nurses' station reminded Joe of bees humming in a hive.

Shifting his weight from one foot to another, Joe noticed his father's eyes were shut tight. Large, bluish bruises covered his arms and cheeks. His tanned, weathered skin was a chalkish white. Joe quickly looked away and moved to the window.

PJ Farris

"Midge?" His father's voice was barely recognizable.

"Yes, Hon, it's me. Joe and your dad are here, too." His mom tenderly patted his dad's arm.

"They operated on my guts early this morning. They'll do more surgery later." His dad coughed and immediately winced. Joe continued to stare out the window.

"That's what the doctor told me. Said you'll be fixed up good as new in no time. Say, these tubes look impressive."

"Yeah. Looks like they're pumpin' expensive water into me." He turned his head slightly. "How's the livestock, Joe?"

"Uh," Joe hesitated.

"Joe?"

"Fine, Dad. Everything's just fine. The cows are fine. So are the hogs. We got some field work done, too." Joe's voiced cracked.

"That's good," was the soft reply. "Sassy calve yet?"

Joe cleared his throat. "No, not yet."

"Watch her close, Joe. She might have trouble, it being her first calf and all."

Joe nodded.

"Joe, you've got lots of work to do. I don't want to hear you've been shootin' hoops instead of doin' the chores."

"The work'll get done, Dad."

"Yes, Son." His dad coughed again. "You'll do the chores and put your basketball away."

Joe's mouth went dry. Tears welled up in his eyes.

Crossover Dribble

Suddenly he needed air, but he didn't dare leave the room.

Don't you understand, Dad, he thought. *Basketball is what I live for! I love basketball! I can work myself to death on the farm and still play basketball in my spare time. The farm work won't suffer. Don't you know how I feel?*

Joe's mom interrupted his thoughts. "Don't you worry about a thing. The farm's running fine. Everything's just fine."

"Sure, Mack. We're getting things done and the weather is supposed to cooperate," Captain said. "Can't do any better than that, you know."

A man dressed in green surgical clothing tapped on the window and Joe's mom left the room.

Captain looked around and asked, "How you feelin'?"

"Terrible."

"That's good cause you look plumb horrible," Captain said.

Joe's dad shot back, "Thanks for the compliment."

"Joe here is a real planter. Bet DeKalb or Pioneer Hybrid will be hiring him away any day now. Why he planted 30 acres today, straighter than a crow flies."

Joe blushed. *It was more like a robin bobbing all over the field,* he thought. *Yet the corn was planted.*

"We'd better let you get some sleep. Joe and I'll get after the soybeans tomorrow. No rest for the wicked, you know."

"Take care, Dad." Joe touched his father's clammy hand.

"You too, Joe. And Joe, I meant what I said."

Chapter 6
Tough Decisions

Heavy traffic slowed their time as they made their way towards home. When the cars and semis had finally thinned out, Joe's mom glanced his way. "The doctor said if everything goes okay with your dad's leg, they'll move him to rehab in a couple of weeks."

Captain said, "That's good news."

Joe simply nodded.

When they pulled up the lane, Captain eased the tension, "I'll rustle up some grub while Joe takes care of the livestock. Unless you want to fix supper, Joe?" he teased.

It wasn't a secret that Joe only knew how to fix peanut butter and jelly sandwiches and grill burgers to a crisp. "No, I'm saving my gourmet recipes for later," he announced.

"If you two can find something to eat, I'll head on out.

Crossover Dribble

Sam's counting on me to work tonight," Joe's mom said.

"We'll be fine," Captain said. "Menu's already set."

Joe rolled his eyes as Captain pretended to stir an imaginary pot.

"And what's that?" Joe asked.

"My specialty—a four-star meal," grinned Captain.

"A four-star meal or a four-alarm heartburn?" Joe's mom quizzed.

"Hey, I'm not sharing my secret recipes with you anymore." Captain acted hurt.

"And Mom won't fix that blackberry cobbler she was talking about," Joe put in.

"Uncle! I give in," Captain said.

"Okay you two. Seriously now, we've got to make some decisions as a family. I know Mack won't like it, but I've decided to try to find a better job," Joe's mom said. "My working part-time at Sam's Quick Stop isn't enough to get us by."

Joe leaned forward. His heart pounded faster as his mom went on.

"And we don't have a dime's worth of medical insurance, so I'll have to see what the state and the hospital will chip in before I know what we'll have to pay. Tomorrow I'm going up to the box factory, and I saw an ad for jobs over at the chemical plant."

"The chemical plant pays well but that's a long drive," Captain said. "How about getting someone to help out on

PJ Farris

the farm, at least until the crops are in? There's too much work for a worn-out old man and a skinny-butt kid."

Joe's face flushed as he squirmed in his seat. *If I was older, I could help out more, like driving livestock to market. It seems like chores Dad did take me twice as long to do, or else I screw up and have to make up for my mistakes.*

"I don't know about extra help, Captain." Joe's mom kept her eyes on the road.

"A young fellow could be a heap of help right now. We're gonna be busier than a one-legged woman in a butt kicking contest," Captain mused.

Finally, Joe joined in, "We just need somebody to help out on weekends, Mom."

"I don't know about the money just yet," his mom said. "Mack had told me he was going to hire extra help for the entire summer, anyway. Now he's going to be laid up for some time. Maybe we could hire a high school boy to work full time. He wouldn't cost as much. What do you think?"

"Sounds good to me. How about Jason Simmons?" Captain asked.

"He's got a job as a stock boy at the grocery store," she said. "Besides, he doesn't like to get dirty."

"You're right. His dad told me he had a job but it slipped my mind. Well, there's Rocky Miller or Alphonso Johnson." Captain turned to Joe. "What about one of them?"

Yeah, put me on the spot, Joe thought. *First you say I'm*

Crossover Dribble

doing a terrific job and then you turn around and say I can't do squat. Sighing, he crossed his arms over his chest. *Now I've gotta come up with someone who can help us,* but he replied, "I heard they're workin' for the county highway."

"Oh, yeah. I heard that at the barber shop last week." Captain pulled a well-worn white hankerchief from his pocket and blew his nose.

"There has to be somebody around," Joe's mom said.

Captain turned to her. "Well, there's Cuda. He's helped us put up hay a couple of times. I don't think he's doing anything, is he?"

Joe's jaw dropped. *Ezekiel Rodriguez, a.k.a. Barracuda, a.k.a. Cuda. Starting guard on the basketball team—the varsity squad, THE TEAM. They won the sectionals last year and might even go all the way to the state finals this year. Cuda's the main cog in the basketball machine. Yeah,* Joe thought, *Cuda knows basketball. But farming? That's different. REAL different.*

Joe's mom perked up, "Mack likes Cuda. Said he's a real good worker."

"Cuda's not exactly the type to make the cover of *Successful Farming*," Joe put in. *Cuda's got a flair for the flamboyant,* Joe thought, *but for farming?* Joe wasn't so sure.

Joe's mom continued, "I remember he's real polite, saying please and thank you. Few of the boys ever do that."

Captain offered, "Cuda likes to work with mechanical

PJ Farris

stuff. Folks say that he can fix about any engine. That'd be handy, and Cuda sure ain't afraid of work."

"Yeah," Joe mumbled.

Cuda's family had been migrant workers until his dad began fixing up the old farm equipment at the produce farm south of town. Now his dad worked as a mechanic at the John Deere dealer and his mom worked as a janitor at the hospital. But Cuda always did the unexpected. If there was trouble at school, Cuda was usually the prime source.

"Cuda helped the Ferguson boys build their barn, didn't he?" Joe's mom asked.

"Yeah, he's a good worker," Joe admitted. "Dad does like him." He didn't add, *despite Cuda's being a basketball player.*

"He's a stout son-of-a-gun. Remember last Halloween? Cuda clumb up the water tower and put a semi-truck tire on top of it. Now that took a lot of muscle." Captain pounded the dashboard with his fist for emphasis.

Joe thought, *all brawn but NO brains. Crazy fool could've fallen off and been killed. And what about Cuda picking up roadkill and depositing it in the wrong places? He tied a dead skunk he'd found to the tailpipe of the principal's car. He got a suspension for three days, and the smell lingered in the car so bad the principal had to get rid of it.*

Joe held his tongue as he thought, *but with Cuda around, there's still a good chance I'll go to camp after all.*

Captain settled it, "I'll call Cuda tonight."

Crossover Dribble

Well, Joe thought, *except for the three-day suspension for the skunk prank, Cuda's got a perfect attendance at school. Likely he'll be dependable. Guess I'll wait and see if he works out.*

Joe stared out the car window at the newly tilled and planted fields. His thoughts of basketball faded with each passing acre.

Once home, Joe's mom changed and dashed off to Sam's while Captain headed to the kitchen.

"Just what *is* the menu, Captain?" Joe asked.

"A surprise," Captain winked. "Now shoo! Go get the chores done and work up a big appetite."

Scottie was glad to see Joe. The dog bounded through the field as he scampered to herd the cattle. Things went smoothly feeding the sows and feeder hogs. Joe gathered the eggs and put the bucket on the porch.

BANG! CLANG!

"Darn it!" Captain shouted from the kitchen.

"Everything all right?" Joe asked as he opened the screen door.

"Sure. Your mom just needs to organize this kitchen better that's all. Cain't find a thing in here."

PJ Farris

"Okay, I'm going out to feed the calves," Joe said.

"Fine. Supper will be ready shortly."

Ambling through the barnyard with Scottie at his heels, the calves stared intently at the two of them. Joe flipped on the electricity, starting the auger, and soon silage flowed down the line of feeders. The calves pushed against each other as they sought out a prime space at the feed bunk for eating.

By the time Joe made it back to the house, the rattling noises from the kitchen had ceased. Joe washed up in the utility room and took in the wonderful aromas wafting from the kitchen. He yelled, "Captain, something smells good! I'm famished."

"Well, prepare yourself, Slats, 'cause you've never had anything like this before."

As Joe opened the kitchen door, he stopped in his tracks. Pots and pans covered the entire counter. Bowls of all sizes were on the table and even on one of the chairs. Eggshells were in the sink, and from the range to the refrigerator to the table, flour dust covered everything.

Captain, with eggyolk and flour splashed across his khaki shirt and pants, proudly pointed to the table. "Fried chicken, mashed potatoes, gravy, and green beans. A feast fit for two kings, namely you and me."

Nodding, Joe slowly turned his head and surveyed the room. "And a mess fit for the whole kingdom."

Looking around, Captain put his hands on his hips and

Crossover Dribble

laughed. "Danged if it's not! Pour a couple of glasses of milk, Joe. We kings better eat before the rest of the kingdom discovers the mess I've made!"

Saturday was usually a day Joe looked forward to, but not this Saturday.

"Why do we have to go to the funeral?" Joe asked.

"Because, he was our neighbor." Joe's mom checked her makeup in the hallway mirror.

"But he nearly killed Dad. For crying out loud, Yeager ran the stop sign and T-boned Dad's truck. The accident was his fault!"

Joe's mom turned and stared him in the eye. "Yes, Joe," she said softly. "It was his fault, and he paid the ultimate price for it. Now his family needs our support. They're going to be paying for his mistake for years, and it wasn't their fault at all."

Ashamed, Joe hung his head. He felt awkward in his dad's oversized white shirt and tie. The starched shirt was scratchy and the tie felt like a noose around his neck about to be tightened at any unsuspecting moment.

Captain was dressed in his navy blue suit, the one he bought for grandma's funeral. Despite the ride to the funeral home taking twenty minutes, no one spoke. The only noise to break the silence was a sneeze by Captain.

PJ Farris

A line stretched outside the funeral home. Joe saw Aaron and Too Tall, students from his class who were with their parents. They nodded and Joe responded. People asked Captain or his mom about his dad. Everyone agreed it was a real tragedy.

The casket was surrounded by bouquets of flowers in bold colors and muted pastels. As Joe followed the visitors through the line, he noticed his hands were clammy. As the organist played "Amazing Grace," Joe watched the Yeager kids and thought, *I could be the one missing a father and sitting on the front row nearest the coffin.*

At the cemetery Joe spoke to the oldest Yeager, a sixteen-year-old boy named Ben. "I'm sorry," Joe said, "really sorry." Nearly a head taller than Joe, Ben looked numb, all emotion drained from his body. Joe wasn't sure if he'd even heard him. The younger kids' reddened faces were tear-stained.

Mom was right, Joe silently realized. *They're the ones paying for their dad's blunder.*

Looking around, he saw his mother and grandfather talking with Mrs. Yeager—a small, blond woman who worked in the school cafeteria, Joe liked her because she was the only lunch lady who ever smiled. Now she looked haggard and lost.

Back in their car, Joe spoke first. "Mom, you were right. We needed to be here," he said softly.

His mom patted his shoulder. "I know, Joe, I know."

Chapter 7
Cuda Arrives

Vroom! Vroom! Vroom! The roar of the old maroon Harley Davidson's motor announced Cuda's arrival. Wearing a black T-shirt, faded Levi's, and high-top sneakers, Cuda's dark brown eyes were concealed behind wrap-around sunglasses. Cuda straddled the bike. A black San Antonio Spurs hat, perched backwards on his head, covered his closely cropped black hair.

"Hola, Mr. Perkins!" Cuda's broad smile yielded perfect white teeth.

"Hey, Cuda! Where'd you get that hat?" Captain asked.

"Found it along the highway. Thought it'd tick folks off if I wore it."

Good grief, Cuda! thought Joe. *Everyone around here is a Bulls or Pacers fan. Why are you always stirring things up?* Joe caught himself and said, "Looks good on ya, Cuda."

"Fits my image. Strong hat, strong man." he said, flexing

PJ Farris

his muscles.

Joe shrugged. *Captain said Cuda's built like a brick house and he's right. If I had his muscles, I'd...*

"We've gotta lot of work to do, Cuda," Captain said.

"Hey, Man, remember I don't feed no pigs and cows! I don't like that stinky stuff on my hands." A sly smile crept over Cuda's face.

"Why, Cuda, you should be used to that 'cause you're full of bullcrap!" Captain shot back.

"No habla English," Cuda grinned.

"No habla English, my foot. You speak English better than I do, but don't worry," Captain said, "you just drive the tractor and take care of the equipment. Joe can feed the livestock and spread the manure."

Yeah, Joe thought, *I'm no grease monkey so I'll gladly shovel manure—chicken, hog, cow, whatever.*

"Well, Joe," Captain asked, "what's up for today?"

Joe took a deep breath. *Thanks, Captain. And thanks for calling me Joe, too.*

Joe's forehead wrinkled as he gathered his thoughts together. Silently, he ticked off a list of tasks in his mind. After a moment, he said, "Cuda can fill the tractors with diesel fuel and check the oil. I'll do the morning feeding. Captain, wanna check on Sassy?"

"Sure."

As they headed off to do their assigned chores, Joe

Crossover Dribble

thought, *the next thing you know I'll be carrying a little notebook and pencil to jot down notes or make lists. Geez, I'm getting to be just like Dad.*

Joe noticed, though, that Cuda dove right into the work. He was impressed.

Now for the tough decision, Joe thought. *Should I let Cuda drive the new John Deere?* Hired hands usually got the oldest machinery to use. *If anything would happen to the new tractor, Dad would give it to me BIG TIME. Captain'd give it to me just as bad. I could drive it. Dad's let me. Hey, I deserve an air-conditioned cab, and listening to CDs would help pass the day away. Cuda does know a heap more about tractors than I do, and he can probably handle it better than I can. Dad always gripes that I drive it like a snail crossing a highway—slowing everything down.*

Captain interrupted Joe's thoughts. "Sassy still hasn't had her calf, but she seems fine. I don't think she's going to calve today."

"The rest of the livestock has been fed and watered," Joe reported.

Cuda spoke up, "The tractors are full of fuel. Only the Ford needed oil. They're all set to go."

"Well, boys, let's get at it!" Captain limped to his pickup.

With a deep breath, Joe took in the sweet smells of the farm. The odors from the feeder calves and newly plowed soil lingered in the air. Slowly, he pointed his finger at Cuda

PJ Farris

and then at the John Deere.

From his perch in the pickup, Captain appeared surprised to see his grandson approach the Ford tractor. Joe gave him a thumbs up and he nodded in reply.

After fiddling with the radio, Cuda put the transmission in gear and eased up on the clutch, pointing the huge green tractor, with its 24-inch disk folded up behind it, down the road.

Following in Captain and Cuda's dusty trail, Joe thought, *I feel like I'm on a little blue hoppy toad with this wimpy four-row planter and a flimsy yellow umbrella for shade. And there sits Cuda in an air-conditioned cab with a soft, comfortable seat. He's singing along with the radio while I'm getting sunburnt and swatting flies. The crop will get in a lot faster this way, but geez, Cuda, I'd like to have it so good!*

The morning of disking and planting went quickly. At lunchtime, they sat down in the shade of the pickup to eat. While Captain brought out the lunch, Cuda demonstrated a basketball maneuver.

"Joe, you know how you see me bust by the guy guarding me? Watch how I do it. I take the ball and dribble with my left hand. Then I keep it low, about at my knees, when I dribble it. Then, boom! I switch to my right hand and turn on the jets and drive to the basket for a lay up!"

"Yeah, that always fools them!" Joe said admiringly.

"Fools them? Joe, a good crossover move takes them out of their defense. Like I broke their rubber ankles, you know?

Crossover Dribble

Let's try it." Cuda pretended to dribble an invisible ball left handed and, keeping his hands low, switched to his right hand and raced past Joe.

"Oh, no fair, Cuda!" Joe smiled. "That's a great move."

"You try it with me," Cuda coaxed.

Joe pretended to crossover from his left to his right hand and back before he raced past Cuda.

"That's it!" Cuda smiled.

"Say, boys, a little practice with the ball back at the house with that trick will pay off this season," Captain observed. "Keeping the ball low like that will help you control the dribble and prevent the guy guarding you from stealing it. And since you're dribbling with either hand, he's not goin' to know which way you're going to the basket, or you can dribble in and kick it out to another player to shoot. Great idea, Cuda!"

"Not my idea, Mr. Perkins. Coach Wilkins showed me how to do it. Says it makes me more flexible."

"And a bigger threat. If a person is flexible and open to ideas, he'll get along just fine. Well, lunch is served fellas." Captain waved his hand toward the pickup bed where he'd laid out baloney sandwiches, potato chips, cups, and a container of iced tea.

"Looks delicious, Captain!" Joe said as he grabbed a sandwich. "I'm so thirsty, I think I could drink a gallon of tea."

"Hey, Mr. Perkins, on the way up to your place, I saw

PJ Farris

Dave Owens and his dad. They had a brand new green thing they were pulling behind the tractor. Looked like a long, rectangular box. Man, was it shiny!" Cuda's eyes sparkled. They always sparkled when he talked about machinery or basketball.

"That's their new drill to plant soybeans," Captain said.

"Don't you drill wheat?" Cuda asked.

"Yeah, wheat and oats. Now, most fellas drill beans, too."

"Won't drilling beans smother the plants, not giving them enough light?" Joe asked his grandfather.

"They don't drill the beans as close together as they do wheat. They adjust the drill to make the rows eight or ten inches apart," Captain said.

"How far apart are you planting the beans, Joe?" Cuda asked.

Is he putting me on, trying to make me look like a fool, or is he for real? Those sunglasses hide his eyes so I can't read him.

"24 inches." Joe's reply was low but firm.

Cuda whistled, "Man, those other farmers are planting two to three times as many beans in their fields as you are! They're gonna need three trucks to your one just to haul their crops in."

Joe winced, but deep down he knew Cuda was right.

"Yeah, I know. But look at it this way, we won't have as long a wait at the grain elevator come fall." Joe knew his joke

Crossover Dribble

was lame. The other farmers would be getting two or three times more money, and money was something they needed.

We can't afford to buy a new drill, Joe thought. *And we can't wait to hire someone to drill the beans because all the farmers with drills plant their own fields first. Our beans would be planted so late they wouldn't have a chance to mature before it frosts. We certainly can't afford that. We barely get by during an average year. Still, it would be a big advantage to plant the beans in narrower rows. But how? There must be some way to make it work. Coach always says use your head.*

Leaning forward, Joe exclaimed, "Hey, wait a minute! Why *can't* we plant the beans in narrow rows?"

Captain looked him squarely in the eye, "No drill, no narrow rows. Simple as that."

"Wait a second! Just give me a chance to explain," Joe enthusiastically pursued his plan. "We're planting our beans 24 inches apart and everyone else is planting them eight inches apart. All we need to do is replant the field so that our rows are 12 inches apart. We'll double our yield!"

Captain stopped chewing on his candy bar. Rubbing his hand over his chin, he mulled over Joe's idea. "That's a lot of extra work."

Joe thought, *stay calm and push this idea across. It'll work! I know it will.*

"Yeah, but we'd double our yield," Joe urged.

PJ Farris

"That'd be pretty risky, you know. We'd need to work longer hours, and if rain set in we might not get all the fields planted."

"Sure, it'll be risky and more work, but we'd have twice the yield at harvest!" Joe was pumped as he got caught up in his idea. "That'd make it a risk worth taking, wouldn't it?"

"Man, you are really using your head, Joe!" Cuda said enthusiastically as he slapped Joe on the back.

See, Captain, even Cuda endorses the idea, Joe thought.

"Come on, Captain, let's try it," Joe pleaded.

"Yeah, Mr. Perkins, you know—be flexible like you said about the crossover dribble."

Slapping his thigh, Captain said, "Okay. We'll give it a go. This isn't a perfect idea, you know. It'll slow us down, and if it rains for more than a couple of days, we'll be way behind. That could mean big trouble. If we have a dry spell we won't be able to cultivate so the plants can get some moisture. We'll be using more fuel for the tractors and have to buy more bean seed, too. It's a real big chance to take, but if it works, Joe, we'll be money ahead come fall. *BIG* money ahead." Captain winked.

Joe leaned back, pleased with himself.

They began replanting the field, putting the new rows in the middle of the ones planted that morning. Cuda and

Crossover Dribble

Captain drove back to the farm to get more soybean seeds while Joe drove the four-row planter.

Coach is right, Joe thought. *Stay calm. Think. Give your best effort, and like Captain says, be willing to try something new. Maybe the crossover dribble idea is worth working on, too.*

As he lowered the planter and eased out the clutch, Joe's thoughts became unsettled. *If the weather changes and the rains come, we might not get the rest of the crop in. No crop, no money. And then what will become of the farm?*

Chapter 8
Sassy Calves

"Joe! Come quick! Sassy's in trouble!" Joe woke from a sound sleep to find Captain shaking him.

"What's the matter?" Joe hastily pulled on a pair of jeans. "I checked her at two this morning and she was fine."

"Well, it's almost six o'clock and she's in trouble. It's a good thing I decided to come over early and check on her. She's trying to have her calf but the calf's too big. She can't push it out." Captain tossed Joe a shirt. "We'll have to pull it."

Shoot! I've never pulled a calf, Joe thought. *I've never even seen it done.*

The sun was rising like a huge red ball over the barn—a magnificent scene that Joe would have paused to absorb any other morning. But this was not the time to take in nature's beauty. "Think we can save it?" Joe asked softly as they walked briskly in the early morning light.

Captain hurried along. "I hope we can, but you never

Crossover Dribble

know. This being Sassy's first calf, we could lose them both. That happens a lot with heifers."

Dust danced in the rays of sunlight that filtered through the slits in the barn planks. Sassy was lying on her side, eyes bulging, bawling in agony.

Dad'll be mad as all get out if the calf dies, and if Sassy dies he'll fill my ears with fireworks and more, Joe thought. *Dang stupid cow!*

"Here, put these on." Captain handed a pair of work gloves to Joe. "You don't want the chain to cut your hands. Grab her tail and I'll hook up the calf puller. Good thing you've got long legs."

"Why?"

"'Cause you'll have to place your feet against her hips and pull the calf out. You'll need the leverage."

"Oh," Joe paused. "What if Sassy stands up?"

"Just hope that she doesn't. Otherwise, get out of the way lickety split or she'll kick the living tar out of you."

Joe looked at Captain then at Sassy. Captain slid a small chain over the calf's feet. Joe's hands trembled as he grasped the calf puller. Similar to a car jack, the device required Joe to brace himself against the cow's hindquarters while he and Captain attempted to ratchet the calf slowly out of the cow. That is, if Sassy cooperated.

"We'll have to pull together. Ready?" Captain asked.

Joe took a deep breath and nodded.

PJ Farris

"Pull like all get out each time Sassy strains to push her calf out," Captain instructed. "You set?"

"Sure." Joe hoped his voice sounded convincing.

"Now!" Captain ratcheted the lever while Joe pulled on the chain. "Pull harder, Joe!"

I can't pull any harder! Joe thought as he gritted his teeth. *Push, Sassy!*

"My arms hurt! I can't pull anymore!" Joe released his hold and looked at Captain.

"Okay, we'll rest a bit," Captain said as he leaned against the wall.

Despite the coolness of the early morning, sweat dripped from their faces. Both of them were breathing hard.

Captain looked at Joe and then Sassy. He asked, again, "Ready? Pull!"

"It's coming!" Joe gasped, "I can feel it move!"

The nose of the calf was scarcely visible. With another pull, the head was out. They gave one last hard tug. Ooof! Sploosh! The calf fell out on the straw bedding. The sound reminded Joe of a rubber boot being pulled from the mud during springtime. A miracle. An absolute miracle!

As Joe unfastened the chain from around the calf's feet, Captain cleaned the mucus from its body with an old towel. Sassy moved her head to look around but failed to get up.

Joe looked at the calf. "Captain, the calf isn't breathing. "Is it...is it dead?"

Crossover Dribble

Dropping to his knees, Joe reached out to the calf. He stroked its body but it didn't move. Captain picked up a long piece of straw and stuck it up the calf's nostrils—first one and then the other. The calf sneezed, causing its sides to expand. Opening its big brown eyes, the calf looked around and bawled, "Moo."

Sassy scrambled to her feet and wandered off to the other side of the barn.

Intently, Joe observed the tiny ribs as the calf began to inhale and exhale. Removing his glove, Joe placed his hand over its heart. "Nice strong heartbeat, Captain."

"Let's stand it up. It'll be a bit wobbly, though."

"Sure." Joe held on to the calf so that it wouldn't collapse and fall.

"Let's help it get a nip of milk for its belly. Saw, Sassy, saw now," Captain spoke as he led the cow to her calf. The calf stumbled and fell. But Sassy ignored it.

"Doggone it," Captain muttered. "She's not going to claim it."

Slowly, Joe picked the clumsy young calf up. Maneuvering it toward the milk dripping out of its mother's udder, Joe said, "Saw, Sassy, saw now." Sassy took one look and stepped aside.

"Now what are we going to do?" Joe asked.

"Feed it on the bottle I guess," Captain answered.

"Great, one more job to do twice a day," Joe muttered.

PJ Farris

"Figures that Sassy would mess up and not want her calf." Joe looked around. "Wait a minute." He went to the feed bunk and got a handful of ground corn mixed with molasses and smeared it over the calf's moist head and back. The grain stuck like yellow glue.

Sassy raised her head.

"Sassy, come and get it girl," Joe coaxed.

Cautiously, Sassy took a small step and let out a low "Moo." Then she moved a bit closer to the calf, sniffing it first before gently licking the feed. The big cow nudged her newborn calf.

"Sassy's discovered motherhood!" Captain said. "Good thinking, Joe." Captain put his hands on his hips and grinned. The calf stood up and nursed on its own, warm milk dripping from its chin. "That calf might've had a difficult time coming out but it knows what to do now."

"Nice calf," Joe said as a warm feeling swept over him.

"A big, healthy, heifer calf, the kind your Dad'll want to keep," Captain replied.

"What a relief! Dad really wanted this calf in the worst way," Joe said. "You saved it, Captain."

"We saved it together, Joe." Captain raised his hand up. Smiling, Joe slapped him a high five.

Chapter 9
Private Lessons

Joe stared out the window. His thoughts were miles away. He'd finishing disking the field, showered, and decided to fix himself something to eat—a masterpiece ham and cheese sandwich on whole wheat along with a tumbler of milk. Seated at the kitchen table, he glanced at the marks on the calendar, "July 8-10 Joe gone to B-Ball Camp."

"Yeah, right," he murmured. Still he didn't want to give up on his dreams.

Joe hadn't picked up the basketball since his father had asked him not to, but that evening, after the chores were done and while his mom prepared a late supper for them, Cuda challenged Joe to a friendly game of one-on-one. Despite the roller coaster ride his emotions had taken all day, Joe's competitive juices began to flow. He was determined to win this contest, or at least put out a good effort trying.

"For Pete's sake, Joe! Play some D! Watch my belly button, not my head. I got you three times on a head-fake." Cuda's eyes danced as Joe took the ball out of bounds.

Okay, Cuda, Joe thought. *Here goes nothing.*

Methodically, Joe stood and bounced the ball between his hands. Using his fingers like the bristles on a paint brush, he stroked the ball back and forth, back and forth. Suddenly, he began to dribble toward the basket with his left hand and then whipped it to his right hand as he put it into high gear to zip past Cuda. Racing full speed, Joe unexpectedly pulled up and took his patented 15-foot jump shot. Swish! Two points!

"Nice going with the crossover, Joe! Now watch this move." Cuda headed toward the bucket. Reversing his dribble, Cuda set up an easy bank shot off the backboard. The ball fell through the rim.

"You blew right by me!" Joe praised Cuda but silently scolded himself. *I knew that crossover was coming.*

"Keep your eyes open, Joe. Watch my middle. My head isn't gonna tell you anything. Check out my stomach, Man."

Cuda dribbled the ball in a steady beat.

With perfect timing, Joe reached in with his right hand, flicking the ball away with his fingertips.

"Man! You've got quick hands!" Cuda shouted as he

Crossover Dribble

tried to catch Joe going in for the lay up.

Joe grinned. "They're not so fast, Cuda."

"I'm telling you they're faster than anyone on our team. Of course, you're not as fast as me." Cuda spoke like Coach often did when he was certain of something.

"Thanks, Cuda." Joe beamed from ear to ear.

"Joe, now I'm gonna make you into a point guard. Pay attention. Keep the ball low and change up your dribble. It's like music. A consistent beat will help the guy steal the ball, so you change the rhythm of your dribble. Confuse him."

"I'll try," Joe said as he practiced dribbling high, then low—slow, then fast.

"That's good. Now work on doing this with the crossover. When the guy looks like you left him behind in wet cement, you make the lay up! Give me the ball. Come here, Man, and watch this." Cuda demonstrated a ball handling drill the high school coach had taught him. He called it the body-circle drill. Cuda quickly moved the ball clockwise around his waist, right knee, left knee, both knees together—right ankle, left ankle, both ankles together—all without letting the ball drop. Cuda lightly touched the ball with his fingertips as it rapidly flew around his body. Joe stood watching, awestruck. Then Cuda reversed the drill and took the ball counterclockwise.

Joe whistled, "Wow! That's fast!"

"Man, I move the ball like this around each part of my

PJ Farris

body 25-30 times every day. I never miss doing it. The other players say they do it every day, but they don't. I know they don't because their hands would move quicker if they did. You need to do this every day." Cuda finished with a big smile. "And work on dribbling. Players should dribble more than they practice shooting, but they don't. They're just ball hogs. They're shooters, not basketball players."

Joe agreed, "Yeah, but it's more fun to score points than to dribble."

"No, Joe, dribbling, passing, and defense are fun, too, you know? Those guys get the big head. They won't ever take a charging foul. I do because I want to be a really good player, not an egomanact."

"A what?" Joe asked.

"You know, an egomanact, a big head," Cuda said pointedly.

"You mean an egomaniac," Joe said.

"Yes! An egnomaniac!" They both burst out laughing.

Joe said, "Let's just call them the big heads."

"Yes," said Cuda, "the big heads, egomanacts!" He continued circling his torso and each leg with the basketball with lightning quick speed.

Captain had been watching the two from the sidelines, and was also astounded with Cuda's ball handling skills. He even offered a bit of advice from time to time. At first, Joe was surprised Captain was encouraging him to play basket-

Crossover Dribble

ball despite his Dad's warning, but he knew Captain had a mind of his own, and, like Joe, he dearly loved basketball.

When the game was over, Cuda grabbed his water jug. He reversed his cap so the visor covered the back of his neck.

"Next time, Joe, I'll show you some fancy passing! See you later!" Firing up his motorcycle, Cuda revved it a couple of times, waved with two fingers, and cruised off down the lane.

As Joe walked to the house, he wondered if he would ever be as good as Cuda, or even good enough to make the starting five.

Chapter 10
Shattered Dreams

On Sunday, Joe's mom left early to work at Sam's Grocery and Gas. After tending to the livestock, Joe treated himself to reading the sports page. Although it wasn't basketball season, sometimes an article about a player or a team snuck in.

At 11:30, Captain picked Joe up and they headed into town to see Joe's dad. They stopped along the way at a restaurant to chow down. Captain ordered his dessert first, something that had always embarrassed Joe's grandmother, but made Joe laugh.

"Life's short," Captain told Joe and the waitress, "and I'd really hate to think I was called by my maker before I had a chance to eat one last slice of banana cream pie or a hot apple dumpling. That'd be an awful thing to have happen to a fella."

Joe's face turned a deep shade of scarlet, but the waitress

Crossover Dribble

just smiled. *After everything that had happened to their family, how could Captain talk so casually about death?*

Joe's dad greeted them as they strolled into the hospital room, "Hey, how are things going with my two hired hands?"

"How are things going with yourself?" Captain countered.

"Not bad. I heard a joke from the nurses. Did you hear about the chicken and the pig? They were talking about the farmer and his wife. The chicken said they were such nice people and took such good care of the animals they should do something for them. The pig said that sounded like a good idea, but what did the chicken have in mind? The chicken said, "We could give them a breakfast of ham and eggs." The pig said, "Hey wait a minute. For you that's a contribution, but for me, that's a major commitment.""

Joe forced himself to laugh despite having heard his math teacher tell the same joke over and over again. He said, "That's a good one, Dad. I brought you some magazines, *Successful Farming* and *Sports Illustrated*."

"Great! That'll help me pass the time, but Joe, you can keep your *Sports Illustrated*. I don't read that stuff." Silently, Joe put the magazines on a table near the bed.

"How are the crops doing? Corn comin' up okay?"

PJ Farris

"Sure," Captain said. "Heck, we ain't amateurs you know. We've got things under control. Don't you fret about that."

"Sassy and her calf doing okay?"

"They're fit as fiddles. That calf looks just like Sassy," Captain replied.

"Yeah, it looks just like her and is just as big a pain in the neck," Joe said. "It started raining a couple of days ago and Sassy headed into the barn. You'd think the calf would follow her, but no. I tried to pick her up..."

"Yeah, and the calf squirmed. When Joe reached for it, he split his britches," Captain hooted.

Joe's dad chuckled. "Sounds like the calf's got lots of spunk. That's good!"

"Joe and I are full of good news. Say, I'm goin' to get a cup of coffee. You two want anything?" Captain asked.

"Nuthin' for me, Dad."

Joe said, "I'll take a soda."

"A soda it is," Captain said as he left the room.

Joe hadn't been alone with his Dad since just before the accident. Shifting his weight, he hoped Captain wouldn't be long. He didn't know what to do, or say. For a while, they both were silent. Then his dad began, "Joe, I've been thinking. There's a lot of work that needs to be done on the farm."

"We're doing all right. Cuda helps out a lot," Joe's voice quivered a bit.

76

Crossover Dribble

"Captain and Cuda can't do it. They don't know what to do."

Joe thought, *most of the time, neither do I.*

His dad went on, "Oh, Captain was a good farmer in his day. But things ain't like they used to be. Farmin's changed a lot. And it keeps changing."

Joe stared at a callous on his hand.

"I've been thinking about this a lot, Joe. There's just too much work for Captain and Cuda. Captain's gettin' along in years, too." His dad cleared his throat. "Joe, I've decided you can't go to basketball camp this year."

Stunned, Joe was silent. He had expected his dad to pull the rug from under his feet but not this soon. Joe clenched his fists. He wasn't going to give up on his dream just yet.

"We have Cuda to help out, and I saved the money and everything!" Joe sounded as though his teeth were tightly clenched together.

"No, Joe. I know how much you were counting on it, but Captain can't do the work alone, and Cuda really doesn't know what to do. And the hospital bills are mounting up, Joe."

Joe looked out the window as tears welled up in his eyes.

Captain walked in and shook his head. "Mack, it's not Joe's fault that you were in the wreck. Things just happen."

"I know, but it's still hard to accept. Maybe I'll never accept it."

PJ Farris

"Maybe you won't, Mack. Let Joe do the camp."

"No, Joe will help you and Cuda."

"But, Dad..."

"You heard me. No basketball camp." Mack pulled up his sheet, dismissing the subject. "That's it. I'm sorry."

A nurse came in with a tray. "Time to start another IV."

"Here's your can of pop, Joe. It looks like we'd best head out for home," Captain said. "We've got chores to do."

"Take care of things," his dad called out as Joe walked down the hallway, his sneakers squeaking with each step on the tile floor. "And Joe, remember, no basketball. The chores need to get done."

Joe kept on walking down the hallway and out the door to the parking lot. On the way home angry thoughts bombarded his brain, ricocheting like a fast game of pinball. His dream was gone—shattered.

Dad didn't want me to go to camp in the first place. Now he has the satisfaction that I'm not going to go at all, Joe thought as he stomped his foot on the pickup's floorboard.

Captain kept his eyes on the road as Joe squirmed on the seat beside him. Finally, Joe leaned on his arm and stared straight ahead.

When they were halfway home, Captain broke the silence, "I don't want you whining and complaining to your mom about not going to camp. Right now she's got a heck of a lot on her mind."

Crossover Dribble

Joe swallowed. His throat felt as though it was packed with sawdust. Feebly he answered, "Yeah, I know."

"There's always next year, Joe. Mack'll be well then." Captain's voice was stern—unusual for him.

Next year, Joe thought. *Next year the guys will be far ahead of my game, and I'll end up as equipment manager, keeping track of tape and washing sweaty uniforms and filthy socks. Yeah, sure—next year!*

"I know, but I really wanted to go to basketball camp. All the good players will be there. Coach says the only way to improve your game is to play better players." Joe pleaded, "Captain, don't you understand?"

Captain didn't respond.

After several miles, he glanced at Joe. "Sure you're disappointed. But everybody gets disappointed, Joe. You think your Dad's pleased about being laid up all summer? Heck, no! Think your Mom's happy about what's happened? We've had lots of hard rows to hoe. Joe, you'll get over it. Life's full of disappointments." He paused. "I know you do what Coach tells you. You want to play against the best players to improve your game, huh? Well, Joe, think you're a better player than Cuda?"

Joe looked at Captain. "Better than Cuda? No way. He's the floor leader of the varsity. Some say he's the best point guard in this half of the state."

"Cuda knows a heap of a lot about basketball, and I was

PJ Farris

a pretty fair ball handler in my day."

Joe shot a quick glance at Captain.

"Don't you think you've sharpened your game since you've been scrimmaging with Cuda?" Captain asked.

"Well, yeah."

"You have to take advantage of situations as they come, Joe."

Silent, Joe became lost in his thoughts.

Okay, maybe my ball handling's improving, and even if Cuda's defense makes me a better shooter, he's just one player. All the good players will be at camp. Captain's no Big Ten basketball coach, either. I don't know if he and Cuda will be enough to help me. I just don't know...

Chapter 11
The Big Storm

The next morning after breakfast, Joe called the university and dropped out of basketball camp. *No use taking up the space that some other guy could use*, he reasoned. *Besides, I won't have to pay the rest of the camp fee.*

Joe and his Grandpa were sitting at the kitchen table a week later when Joe's mom announced, "The doctor says Mack needs more surgery and more weeks in traction."

Joe couldn't believe it. "But he's already been in there over two weeks!"

"Yes, I know. The doctor said the surgery on his leg went well, but it's not healing right. He'll have surgery again on Wednesday, and then they'll move him to the rehab center for another month." His mom paused before going on, "I know it's a big jolt for everyone—this news and the fact that

PJ Farris

I still haven't found a steady job. I wish that box factory position would come through for us. The bills are really adding up. I know the two of you are just plain worn out. I'm even worried about Cuda, as tough as he is. I just don't know what to do." She turned, leaned on the kitchen sink and stared out the window. The young calves were playing in the pasture as their mothers grazed nearby.

I don't know if I can last, Joe thought. *My body aches and I'm so tired I can't remember things.*

Refilling his coffee cup, Captain stirred in milk and sugar. Finally, he spoke, "We're getting along fine, just fine. If Mack needs to be in traction, that's where he should be." Captain was taking the news in stride just as Joe knew he would. "Besides, Slats," Captain said as he tickled Joe's ribs, "if your dad was able to be out and about, he'd be itching to help us."

"Yeah," Joe replied.

Captain winked at him. "All this happening just when we're revolutionizing this farm and getting it in shape. Better to keep him in a hospital bed than to have to hogtie him to the house."

Shrugging his shoulders, Joe said, "I guess so." He glanced worriedly at his mother. "Well, time to do the feeding." He pushed his chair back from the table and went to the back porch. He pulled on his worn sneakers, gave Scottie a pat, and walked slowly to the barn. With a wary

Crossover Dribble

eye, Joe examined the clouds. The sky had looked threatening all afternoon and had now darkened into deep blues and purples.

"We'd better hustle, Scottie. Rain's a comin'!"

Without wasting time, Joe and Scottie quickly brought the cows in. As Joe fastened the barnyard gate, rain began falling in huge drops. Running beside Scottie to the farrowing house Joe noticed the sky had turned to black, fooling the automatic nightlight as it lit up the barnyard in the darkness. A gust of wind whipped a loose sheet of aluminum roofing on the tool shed causing it to bang up and down.

Searching the sky for a funnel-shaped cloud, Joe muttered, "That's all we need. A tornado to wipe out the house or barn." Scottie nudged against his leg. "It's okay, fella." Joe patted Scottie's wet fur and watched from the barn door at the progressing storm. "I'm a bit scared myself. I wonder how Mom and Captain are doing. The house is built better than this old barn, Scottie. A real good wind could blow this whole thing away."

Lightning flashed and cracked, striking a tree in the woods. SNAP! BOOM! Joe chewed on a fingernail as Scottie fidgeted nervously at his feet.

The temperature dropped quickly, causing goose bumps to form on Joe's arms. Hail hit the metal roof with a sound of a timpani drum. The sows and pigs grunted and squealed. The storm roared on. Joe looked out at the barnyard in disbelief.

PJ Farris

"Well, Scottie," Joe said disgustedly, "this about does it. I can't go to basketball camp after working my rear end off for two years to save up for it. Now this hailstorm will wipe out all the crops!"

From the barn he watched as hail beat his mom's tomato plants into the ground. Joe knew the same thing was happening to the corn out in the fields—pelting it until the small shoots broke.

Rubbing Scottie's wet head, Joe thought, *all that work and the good start the crops have gotten off to will be lost—wiped out. It's not fair, not fair at all!*

Tears flowed down his cheeks as Joe buried his head in Scottie's fur, his arms wrapped around the dog's neck. The hail was followed by large drops of rain that pummeled the aluminum roof like a child throwing handfuls of marbles on a piece of tin. Scottie began licking Joe's face.

"It's okay, Scottie." Joe inhaled the rain-freshened air and calmed himself. "Come on, fella. Let's get some chores done."

Eagerly, Scottie jumped to his feet and headed for the feed bin in the barn. Joe fed the sows and watered them before creep feeding the baby pigs. Resting on some feed bags with Scottie at his feet, they waited out the storm. For several minutes the rain fell in silver sheets as the wind blew with ferocity. Joe tossed pebbles at a bucket to kill time. Glancing at the dog, he murmured, "At least you appreciate

Crossover Dribble

me, Scottie. You'll just have to watch me shoot hoops in the barnyard. Maybe I can make the starting five if I work hard enough. Maybe that crossover dribble move will improve my game and kick it up a notch. Maybe, just maybe..."

When the rain slackened, Joe and Scottie made a mad dash to the house where his mom and Captain were watching the TV weather report.

"Tornado touched down north of here near the county line. Did you see any funnel clouds out there?" Captain asked.

"Nope. Sounded like lightnin' hit a tree up in the woods, though." Joe took off his drenched T-shirt and dropped it into the washer.

"We heard that and were worried about you and Scottie," his mom said. "It was one humdinger of a storm."

"That's putting it lightly," said Captain. "Well, better go see just how bad things are. You check the fence rows for downed limbs. I'll go check the corn. That hail likely destroyed it." Captain reached for his old green cap.

Shivering as he buttoned his plaid cotton shirt, Joe said, "I'll go with you. I can check the fence later this afternoon."

As they drove along the country roads, muddy water raced in brown rivulets through the fields to the waiting ditches. Dots of ice clung to grass in the waterways, the white particles in stark contrast to the dark, wet soil.

"Oh, no!" Joe gasped leaning out the window in dismay.

PJ Farris

"Looks like it's been hit by a food chopper," Captain said.

Joe shook his head in amazement. "There's not a single plant left standing," he said, feeling somewhat nauseous. His dad had planted the corn three weeks before the wreck. Corn that had been a foot high with deep green leaves only this morning, was now lying beaten down in mud.

Horrified, Joe asked, "What'll we do now?"

"The only thing we can do. Buy more seed and replant." As Captain eased his foot off the brake, the pickup crept along, Joe's eyes glued to the field.

"We'll only have to buy corn seed with a short season, like they plant up in Minnesota or Wisconsin," Captain said.

"Can't we plant soybeans? They have a shorter growing season," Joe offered.

"Naw. The herbicides sprayed on the field for the corn would kill the soybeans. We've no choice but to replant."

They drove along slowly and examined field after field. Recently planted crops were not damaged because the corn was too small to be hurt. The same was true of the soybeans. With a nod, Captain grunted his approval at the slight damage they had encountered.

"We've come through it better than I thought, Slats. Could've been worse."

Joe nodded.

When they got to the north twenty, Joe lacked the

Crossover Dribble

courage to survey the damage. That was the first field he had ever planted himself. *Could it be that all that work was for nothing?*

"Last field, Joe." Captain slowed the truck to barely a roll, then brought it to a halt.

"What do you think?" Joe asked nervously.

"Looks like it got the full bore of the storm. It'll have to be replanted. Tough luck, Joe."

"Yeah, tough luck. My whole summer can be summed up as tough luck." Joe grimaced.

Captain turned to face him. "You've taken a couple of hard blows, Joe, but you're not the only one. Take a look around."

Joe remembered how his dad squeezed as much grain as possible out of Widow Conner's fields so she'd have some income to help stretch her meager social security checks. And he thought about his dad and the Yeager family.

"Sorry, Captain. It's just that I'm frustrated."

"Anything else?" Captain asked.

"Yeah, I'm feeling sorry for myself."

"Most people do at one time or another, Slats. You can't spend your whole summer down in the dumps. Got to get on with things."

Reluctantly, Joe nodded in agreement.

Captain went on, "Say, let's go by my place and fetch a tarp and some plywood to put the seed corn on to keep it dry.

PJ Farris

Then we'll run by Jim Morgan's and pick up the short-season seed corn. Tomorrow morning there'll be a rush to buy it." Captain pulled onto the paved road.

"Dad doesn't like to charge it. How will we pay for it?" Joe asked.

"Is there any money left in the checking account?"

Joe shook his head. He and his mom had spent the previous evening going over bills—feed, utilities, medical—there were far more bills than the money would stretch. Joe asked, "How much will it cost?"

Captain calculated in his head. "It'll take sixteen bags of seed corn to redo the two fields. That'd run about three hundred and fifty dollars, maybe a little more."

Inhaling slowly as though trying to inflate an oversized balloon, Joe sat stonefaced. "Stop by the house. I've got the money."

Captain gave Joe a questioning look.

"Don't worry," Joe swallowed hard, his voice sounding raspy, "it's the money I saved for basketball camp."

Chapter 12
Trouble With Sassy

Early the next morning Joe and Captain patrolled the fence rows, discovering the storm had knocked down several limbs. A large branch from a sycamore tree had fallen across the fence and the cows had already noticed. Never passing up an opportunity, they found the neighbor's hayfield enticing and jumped across the downed fence into the pasture. Sassy even left Rosebud behind to gorge herself on fresh red clover.

"That Sassy is one stupid beast! She's got no mothering instinct at all," Captain fumed. "First it's one dang thing, then another."

Joe was puzzled. This wasn't like Captain at all. Ever the optimist, he tended to shake things off with a joke or a grin. Then Joe noticed how tired his grandfather looked, his face was a bit ashen.

"This wouldn't have happened, Joe, if you'd checked

PJ Farris

the fence after the storm like I asked you to. I'm tired of having more and more work to do when there's no reason for it." Captain's cold blue eyes were piercing.

"I'm sorry, Captain. I guess with the corn getting hit so bad and all, I forgot. It won't happen again. I promise."

"It darn well better not," Captain sputtered. "Use your noggin next time." Captain looked at Joe, then off into the distance, and sighed. "I reckon I could've reminded you. Ah, well, what's done is done. Scottie, go get around them."

Like a shot, the black and white dog went through a small hole in the fence and rushed through the red clover. Fortunately, the cows hadn't been in the hayfield long. The neighbor helped Joe and Scottie chase the wayward cows back into their meadow.

"Don't worry about it, Joe," the neighbor said. "They didn't do much damage. The hailstorm hurt the field more. Say, how's your dad doing?"

"He's coming along fine. They say he'll be home before we know it." Joe said. "Thanks for helping us round up the cattle. I promise they won't get out again."

Shouldn't promise, he thought. *Sassy's nothing but trouble.*

The small chain saw under Captain's steady hands quickly cut up the limbs while Joe carried them away. As they mended the fence, Captain warned, "We'd better keep a close eye on them the next day or so."

"Sure," Joe replied as he picked up the tools.

Crossover Dribble

The next morning, Joe let the cattle out of the barnyard. As if drawn by a magnet, the herd quickly went back to where the limb had fallen. But Joe and Captain had the fence tightly secured, leaving the cattle no choice but to amble out to pasture.

One of the cows lingered in the barnyard. Joe climbed up on a gate to check it out. The cow's stomach was blown up like a helium balloon and she could barely move. Inwardly, Joe groaned. "Not again." It was his dad's favorite cow and Joe's favorite nemesis—Sassy.

"That doggone cow can't do anything right!" Joe threw his hat down on the ground and climbed down. Picking up his hat, he tugged it down on his head and went to the house to fetch Captain.

After carefully surveying the animal, Captain seemed worried. "If we don't do something for her quick like, she'll die before long." His voice was edgy, "I should've figured one of them would bloat, with all the red clover they ate."

"She deserves to die." Joe's voice sounded harsh.

"Nothing deserves to die, Joe," Captain replied. "She's certainly got herself in a heck of a mess. She's one sad lookin' critter."

Feet sprawled apart, Sassie's head hung down. She was breathing heavily.

"If you'd checked the fence like you were supposed to, she wouldn't be in this mess! Go call the vet and see if he

PJ Farris

can come!" Captain barked at Joe.

Joe turned and began walking out of the barnyard toward the house. Captain yelled, "Hurry up! We ain't got all day! Run, boy, run!"

With some coaxing of the cow by Scottie, Captain managed to lead Sassy into the barn and put her in a long abandoned milking stanchion.

After calling the vet, Joe ran back. "She give you much trouble?" he asked.

"Heck no, she's in misery! What did the vet say?"

"His wife answered the phone. He'll be here in an hour or so."

Captain snorted, "For crying out loud, Joe, by then she'll probably be dead!"

"What'll we do?" Joe asked.

Captain pondered aloud, "If your dad was here, he'd take a knife and stick her."

"Stick her?"

"Yeah, stick her. He'd take a butcher knife and stab her with it in the side and the gas would escape. He's saved several cows that way. Remember two years ago? He saved that Johnson boy's 4-H calf that bloated on sweet clover in early May. That calf went on and took second place at the fair that summer."

Joe did remember. He also remembered that his dad told him you always stick the animal between the third and

Crossover Dribble

fourth ribs. *Or was it right in the stomach?* He couldn't recall for certain—and the wrong spot could be fatal.

"I'll get the butcher knife so you can stick her," Joe offered.

"Joe, your dad knows how to do it. I don't." Captain paused and turned to look Joe in the eye. "Did he ever tell you anything about doing it?"

Eyes lowered, Joe appeared to examine his sneakers before confessing, "Yeah, but I didn't pay enough attention."

A sudden emptiness filled Joe, as if he was taking a math test but he didn't recognize how to do any of the problems.

"We could call Dad," Joe suggested.

"And he'd hit the ceiling! Besides, they don't want him upset." Captain put his hands on his hips. Sassy let out a mournful bellow.

"She's in bad shape, Joe. We've got to think of something—and pronto! She's filling up with air faster than a balloon. If we don't help her soon, we'll lose her," Captain said as he leaned on a pitchfork in the straw. Scratching his head, he said, "You know, if we could get her to belch, she'd be okay until the vet comes."

"How can we do that?"

Captain paused and asked, "What makes you belch?"

Joe thought a second and spouted, "Your homemade chili." Joe grinned.

"Yeah," chuckled Captain. "A lot of good that'll do us.

PJ Farris

You know, Joe, I do remember something about giving a cow vegetable oil, but I'm not sure..."

Something clicked in Joe's brain. "I'll be right back!" he called over his shoulder.

As Joe raced to the house the wet grass caused his sneakers to slip and he stumbled, but quickly righted himself and ran on. Picking up three plastic bottles of Coca Cola and a bottle of cooking oil, he ran back just as fast. Sassy rolled her eyes and stepped sideways as he rushed into the barn.

"Don't scare her, Joe! She's going to be hard enough to handle the way she is!" Captain warned.

Joe put the bottle of oil between his legs. He wired a wooden gate tightly confining the cow in the stanchion next to the wall. Satisfied that Sassy couldn't move, Joe held her head and sloshed vegetable oil down her throat, followed by the three bottles of cola. Sassy, deciding she'd had enough, attempted to swing her head away.

"Well, what do you think?" Joe asked.

Captain took his hat off and scratched his head. "I don't know. How long before you think it should work?"

"When I guzzle down pop real fast, I usually belch right away," Joe answered, "but I don't know about cows."

"Let's wait a spell and see what she does."

Sassy stared at them, her eyes glassy.

"Maybe the gate's putting too much pressure on her sides. Let's move that," Captain said.

Crossover Dribble

Joe bent down to unwire the gate. As he stood up, Sassy raised her head and gave an enormous belch right in his face.

"I'll be. It worked!" Captain shouted, "That's a sure-fire remedy, Joe! Keep her moving so she can walk it off."

Sassy belched again and again as Joe led her around the stall several times. The putrefied odor from the gas Sassy gave off filled the barn. Leaning on the cow, Joe bent over and vomited.

Captain reared back his head and laughed. "If that don't beat all! Some vet you'd make, Slats!" He handed Joe his red handkerchief.

Joe went over to a water hydrant and moistened the handkerchief before wiping his face with it. "That smell is awful! No wonder bloated cows die!" Joe sat down on a manger and sighed.

"Well, you saved her life, Joe. And you saved her calf, too. Why, you're Sassy's guardian angel!"

"Don't go and pin that on me, Captain. She hates me."

As if in agreement, Sassy stretched out her neck and let out a gigantic belch, once again filling the barn with a malodorous odor. Joe and Captain pushed and shoved each other trying to get outside into the fresh summer air.

Chapter 13
Another Lesson

Later that afternoon, Joe went out to do the chores. Scottie had the routine down pat, going first to the chicken house and then to the pasture to bring in the cows. Joe watched him thinking, *Scottie could bring those darned cows in by himself. That would sure save me some time.*

When he went into the kitchen, his mother met him with a big smile on her face. "Good news, Joe! I got the job down at the box factory!"

"Terrific, Mom!" He gave her a hug, happy and relieved at the same time.

"I go to work Monday morning in the office." she beamed. "I'm planning on still working weekends for Sam, maybe even one evening a week. That'll help pay off the bills a lot sooner."

"That's good news, real good news," Captain said. "Joe and me have an appetite the size of the Grand Canyon.

Crossover Dribble

What's for supper?"

"Something sure smells good!" Joe peered into the oven. "Mmmmm! Meatloaf!"

The chatter and laughter around the kitchen table was a pleasant change from the solemn discussions of the previous weeks. Captain told about Cuda watching the cattle graze early one morning while dew still glistened on the grass. With a twinkle in his eye, he said, "I hollered at him. 'Hey, Cuda! It's good luck to spit over an electric fence!' Cuda said, 'Yeah, Man? Well, I need some luck.' Cuda filled his mouth with spit and aimed a big stream at the neighboring pasture."

Captain slapped his thigh and laughed, "You should've seen Cuda dance! He yelled and jumped around, screaming at me all the while he was holding his tongue with his fingers."

Joe's mom said, "You ought to be ashamed of yourself, Captain. That was a dirty trick to play on Cuda."

"I told him, 'sometimes spitting over an electric fence is luckier than other times!'" Captain laughed.

Joe retorted, "Cuda is good about playing tricks on us, Mom. When Captain took his shoes off for his afternoon nap, Cuda tied them together and tossed them up into the oak tree in the front lawn. It took Captain twenty minutes to figure out how to get them down.

"Then Captain retaliated a few days later by completely encircling Cuda's beloved motorcycle with hog manure.

PJ Farris

"Cuda yelled, 'Hey, Man, that's my Harley! That's not a piece of rusty old farm machinery. It's a sweet machine!'"

Joe went on, "Of course Captain was sitting on the porch sipping iced tea. 'Well, Cuda, if you ride it through that manure pile, it won't be a sweet machine for long. You'll both stink worse than a skunk!'

"Then Cuda goes poking around and comes back with an old rotted railroad tie. He dragged all 150 pounds of it over to his motorcycle, drove the Harley up onto the railroad tie, and headed for home—the motorcycle as clean as a whistle. Cuda was laughing his head off!"

Captain said, "That Cuda's sure strong! I thought I'd gotten the best of him!"

"Another time he stole your hat and tied it to the top of the sun umbrella on the Ford tractor. It took you all day to find it," Joe laughed.

"Neither one of us could figure out how Cuda accomplished that feat. I never even noticed him taking it." Captain shook his head and chortled.

Joe grinned, "You didn't notice him stealing your hat 'cause you were catchin' 40 winks in the pickup."

Joe's mom joined in the laughter.

"Cuda's a lot of fun," Joe said.

"And one hard worker," Captain chimed in.

"Good thing he's got a sense of humor and a strong back, keeping up with the two of you and your shenanigans," Joe's

Crossover Dribble

mom said as she put the carrots, corn, and mashed potatoes on the table.

Captain buttered a slice of bread. "When you going up to see Mack?"

"Tomorrow after I get off work at Sam's. I talked with him on the phone just before you two came in—two pieces of meatloaf, Joe?"

"Sure. Did Dad say how he was doing?"

"He's doing fine. He fusses that they make him work too hard at the rehab center. I think he's looking forward to coming home," his mom said as she passed the platter.

Joe relaxed and leaned back in his chair. He thought, *maybe things are turning in our favor. Just maybe...*

Early Saturday morning, Joe heard the car roar off down the lane as his mom went to work at Sam's. He got dressed and went to the kitchen where he fixed himself a large bowl of corn flakes and a glass of orange juice. After chowing down, he went out to do the morning chores. While Cuda had Saturdays and Sundays off, the farmwork continued for Joe. On weekend mornings Joe shot baskets and practiced his dribbling, but only after the livestock had been taken care of.

Coach tells us that practicing when you're tired builds stamina and heart. By Saturday, I'm drained, Joe thought. *No gas left in the tank!*

PJ Farris

Like a diehard fan, Scottie watched from the sideline.

Another frequent observer was Captain, who would give a suggestion or two. He often reminded Joe to use the backboard when he shot. "Bank it, Joe!" he'd say. Or sometimes he'd yell, "Square up your shoulders to the basket before you shoot!" Or "Bend your knees! Shoot with your legs! That's where the power comes from."

Inside, Joe would moan, but he knew Captain was right.

"Come on, Joe! What do you think you're doing? Shooting free throws or pretending to be a windmill? Keep that elbow close to your body!" Captain fussed and fumed. "And follow through, Joe. The shot's not finished until you follow through. Pretend you're putting your hand in the basket at the end of the shot."

Joe nodded and followed his instructions.

"Now the player guarding you will tend to take a head fake. If you fake with both your head and your shoulders, chances are you'll be able to get him to commit—get him to jump at the wrong time. Then you've got an opening to take a shot." Captain demonstrated a head and shoulders fake in slow motion. Joe nodded and tried it.

"Don't forget that most players watch your eyes, Joe. If you look away, that'll throw them off balance. Then you can either shoot or drive past them."

Footwork and ball handling had been Captain's specialties as a player. He showed Joe how to be a triple threat.

Crossover Dribble

"Just put your shooting foot slightly ahead of your other foot when you land after a rebound or catching a pass. Then you can either pass the ball, shoot it, or drive to the basket."

"That's something Coach tells us," Joe said.

A superb passer in his day, Captain showed Joe how to do two-handed overhead passes, bounce passes, and chest passes. He even showed him how to perfect no-look passes. Captain said, "Slats, the better you can pass, the more you'll free up your teammates and help your team. Just find the open man, and bang! Your team will score a bucket!"

They practiced passing on Saturday and Sunday evenings until it got too dark to see the ball. On those nights, Joe fell into bed exhausted but happy.

Chapter 14
The Contest

"You fellas have us all caught up," Captain said as he sat on a bale of straw and watched Joe and Cuda go over the equipment. "Fair starts Thursday. You boys could have yourselves a good time there."

"But we've got work to do," Joe protested. "Cuda can go. I'll stick around and get the chores done."

"Naw," Captain handed a bolt to Cuda. "Nuthin' is pushing us right now."

The replanting hadn't been as bad as anticipated. As Cuda disked the fields, Joe and Captain followed and planted the corn making short work of it. Then they cultivated the weeds out of the corn in the fields that hadn't been damaged by the hail. Captain was pleased and so was Joe. They spent the next two weeks mowing fence rows and waterways as well as repairing equipment. Under Captain's watchful eye, Joe broke some of the young calves to lead. The trips to

Crossover Dribble

town were less frequent. Daily phone calls to the rehab center reassured Joe's dad that things were going well and time wasn't being wasted.

Fumbling with the pocket of his bib overalls, Captain pulled out his worn leather wallet. "Tell you what. I'll give you each ten dollars to spend. How does that sound?"

"Great!" Cuda and Joe said in unison. They looked at each other and laughed.

"Well, I'd best be heading home," Captain said. "I haven't seen the farm report for a week. I'd better see what the market's up to. Might even wander out to the hammock and check my eyelids for holes."

Picking up the lube gun, Joe began squirting grease into the tiny nozzles on the big disk while Cuda watched.

"Man, how about you and me entering the Farm Hand Contest?"

Joe put down the lube gun. "Are you kidding? Haven't you heard of the pig catching part? You'll have to get your hands dirty, Cuda."

"Sure, Man, but we could take that contest," Cuda flashed a big smile. "First prize is $500—$250 for each of us."

Joe whistled, "$250. That's a lot of money."

Cuda grinned, "I thought you'd say that."

The Farm Hand Contest had been started as a way to promote the local implement dealers. They wanted to convince farmers to take better care of their tractors so they would buy more parts and lubricant. Then the feed store owners suggested adding events that dealt with livestock. In the end, the Farm Hand Contest consisted of teams of two teenagers competing together for cash prizes.

"Are you sure, Cuda? I mean, do you want to toss manure?"

"Dry manure washes off with soap and water. Wet manure makes you stink."

"Well, I'm willing if you are." Joe reached out his hand and Cuda slapped it.

The Farm Hand Contest consisted of five events. The first was the tractor repair event. Each team was given a tractor with a minor mechanical problem to solve. The winner was the first team to get its tractor started and drive it across the finish line. Local implement dealers furnished the tools and parts the teams needed to make the repairs.

"Cuda, this is your event, not mine," Joe murmured as they stood at the starting line. Facing them were a series of old tractors with a variety of mechanical difficulties. "They all look like they belong in a junkyard," Joe observed.

"Shhhhh! Older tractors are easier to fix, Joe. Just stay alert and look for the problem. I'll do the rest." Cuda's eyes flashed in anticipation.

Bang! The starter's pistol startled Joe for a moment. They

Crossover Dribble

ran as fast as they could to an ancient Massey Ferguson.

"Should be a piece of cake, Joe. These tractors are a lot like Captain's old Ford," Cuda said as he attempted to start the engine.

Joe looked the tractor over. "Hey, it's got a battery and its charged up," he said.

"Shhh! Not so loud, Joe," Cuda scolded.

Joe's face reddened as he heard one of the members of the neighboring team tell his partner to look at the battery.

"Crawl under the tractor, Joe. See if you can find anything."

"Okay." Joe dropped to the ground. "What should I look for?"

"Loose wires, missing spark plugs, anything." Cuda went over the engine inch by inch.

"Crud! Somebody must have taken a leak under here," Joe muttered. "Now I'm all wet!"

"Wait! Where was it?"

Joe pointed to the ground. Cuda grinned as he grabbed a towel and screwdriver.

"Good news, Joe! Nobody took a leak. They just poured water over the distributor cap. I'll dry it and the points off. You get on the seat and start 'er up. I'll hop on back and you can drive it across the finish line."

Cuda nodded to Joe who turned the key on and pushed the starter button. Vvvvrrrrooooommmmm! Cuda jumped

PJ Farris

on the tow bar and Joe put it into fifth gear. They sped across the finish line just before the team of Too Tall and his older brother, Nate, drove an old orange Case tractor over the line. To the crowd's delight, third place went to Brittany Adkins and Jaime Jeffers, the only all-girl team in the contest.

Joe turned to Cuda and said, "That's a relief!"

"What, Joe?" Cuda said with a laugh. "Winning the event or knowing you aren't wearing a T-shirt filled with pee?"

They both chuckled.

The next event was the hay-stacking contest. A stack of 24 bales of hay had to be moved and restacked 30 feet away. The team members took turns on this event. Joe and Cuda drew number seven. They watched as the first six teams stacked and restacked the bales.

"Too bad we didn't get a lower number," Joe said.

"Yeah, Man. By the time we get to the bales, they'll be loose from having all the hayhooks stuck in them."

Cuda was right. When Joe reached for a bale with his 18-inch hayhook, he found he had to stab twice before it caught because the hay wasn't held together tightly. Even when he tried to grab the bales by the twine wrapped around them, they nearly came undone. Finally the last bale was moved and placed on top of the stack.

"Done! Nine minutes and 46 seconds!" called the judge.

Joe looked at the board. *Well,* he thought, *there are still three events left.*

Crossover Dribble

Too Tall and Nate were the last team. Between them, they weighed over 400 pounds. Nate took two hayhooks, one in each hand, and raced toward the haystack. In one fluid motion, he sank the hooks deep into two bales and began dragging them.

How can you beat that? He's a regular hay-stacking machine! Joe thought as he checked the clock.

Trip after trip, Nate dragged two bales while his brother dragged one. It was as if they had three members, not two.

Then, Cuda nodded to Joe. Nate had started on the final bales when one of the bales doubled up and broke, spreading hay across the floor.

"Broken bale! Two minute penalty!" shouted the judge.

"Yes!" Joe whooped. They were in second place.

The next event was the cowpie toss. Dried cow manure was tossed like a discus throw. The winner would be the team with the longest throw.

"This is my event, Joe," Cuda said confidently.

"Yeah, but Charley Johnson's in it, and he's the pitcher on the baseball team."

"Doesn't matter. This is like flipping a Frisbee, only cowpies are heavier. It's all in the wrist." Cuda motioned.

"All right. I think I can do that." Joe wasn't sure though. This time they drew the second position.

"Get the flattest ones, Joe."

Joe picked out three flat, circular cowpies. His first toss

PJ Farris

was 27 feet. Then he heaved one 42 feet.

"Come on, Man! Get into it!" Cuda shouted.

Grasping the dried circle of manure, Joe flipped it out 57 feet, his best effort, and the one that would count for the team.

Slowly Cuda crossed his right arm to his left hip and then whipped the cowpie into the air. It landed 64 feet away.

"Nice toss, Cuda!" someone shouted from the crowd. Cuda took a bow.

Cuda took aim with his second attempt. With a nifty flip the cowpie ended up 79 feet away. The crowd cheered and Cuda took another bow.

Cuda, come on. We don't have time for you to show off, Joe thought. *We still have a chance to win this!*

On his third attempt, Cuda paused and then heaved the cowpie. The toss went awry, hitting a bystander in the head.

"Sorry!" Cuda yelled. The crowd laughed as the high school principal brushed manure off his shirt.

"Cuda! What are you doing?" Joe was appalled.

"It slipped, Man. It just slipped. Honest. Besides," Cuda's eyes danced, "he can't suspend me from school now. It's summer vacation."

Nate wound up and spun a cowpie out 79 1/2 feet. Joe and Cuda both groaned. But then Charley Johnson heaved a toss of 103 feet.

"We've still got a chance, Joe" Cuda said.

Crossover Dribble

"A slim one," Joe answered solemnly. "Let's hope we can win the next two events."

The fourth event was the wheelbarrow race. The course was twice around the midway, switching riders at the halfway point. Cuda sat in the wheelbarrow ready to go.

"Okay, Joe. Stay steady and don't wobble. If you try to go too fast, you'll toss Cuda out on his ear," Captain directed.

"Listen to your grandpa, Joe. I don't want to get run over." Cuda reiterated.

"Get on your mark. Get set." Bang! The judge fired the gun into the air, but Joe was ready this time. Digging his heels in, he started pushing the wheelbarrow toward the Ferris wheel. Too Tall was right behind him with Nate inside the wheelbarrow.

"Oh, Man! Take it easy! Those ruts and hoses are hurting my buns!" Cuda called out.

"Just hang on!" Joe grunted as they sped around the roller coaster. Down the length of the midway they flew, passing the ring toss and haunted house.

"Hey, Man! We're ahead!" Cuda encouraged, "Faster, Joe!"

Turning the corner past the tilt-a-whirl, Joe guided them back to the starting line. The race was half over and they were still in the lead.

Cuda jumped out as Joe fell into the wheelbarrow. They were off again! Down to the Ferris wheel and over the elec-

PJ Farris

trical hoses by the roller coaster. Thud! Thud! Joe hung on tight as he was jostled back and forth and from side to side, his teeth rattling in his head.

Nate gave Cuda a threatening look. Whether Cuda caught it or not, Joe didn't know. Just then the wheelbarrow with Too Tall inside came up next to them. Nate was trying to cut them off by the ring toss.

"Move over!" yelled Too Tall.

"Get over yourself!" Joe barked back.

The wheelbarrows bumped together, pinching Joe's fingers. Wincing with pain, he held on.

"Come on, Cuda!" Captain shouted.

Putting on the afterburners, Cuda hustled down the stretch with just enough speed to cross the finish line first.

"Way to go, fellas!" Captain shouted amidst the cheers of the crowd.

After four events, they were tied with Too Tall and Nate. The only event left was the toughest one—the greased pig race. Each team member had to catch a greased pig and pull, push, or persuade it into the team's pigpen.

"Joe, you were right." Cuda said as he surveyed the arena where the greased pig race was to take place.

"About what?" Joe questioned.

"I was crazy to have us enter this contest. Man, just look at that arena. You can't even stand up in that stuff."

Joe had to agree with Cuda. After the first four events

Crossover Dribble

they now had to go out and wrestle 50 pound pigs that had enough cooking oil on them to fry a week's worth of french fries at a McDonald's, and they had to do it in the arena where the mud wrestling contest took place the night before. They'd be up to their knees in mud.

"Hey, Man!" Cuda jerked his head. "Come with me!" he shouted.

Cuda started running and Joe followed close behind.

"Where are we going?" Joe called.

"To the bridge!"

Cuda slid down an embankment to the stream. Putting his arms in the water to wet them down, he then rolled in the sand along the bank.

"Come on, Joe! We can't waste any time!" Cuda yelled.

Following Cuda's lead, Joe waded in the water and moistened his hands and arms before covering them with sand.

Cuda grinned. "Let's go catch us some pigs!"

Joe laughed and called, "Soooooowwwwweeeeee!"

People in the crowd chuckled and pointed at Cuda and Joe, but Cuda didn't give them any notice. The judge dropped a flag and thirty 50-pound, shiny pigs bolted through the mud followed by a swarm of Farm Hand contestants. The pigs ran, splattering contestants and any observers who had gotten too close to the fence.

Joe targeted a red pig with long ears that looked promis-

PJ Farris

ing. *At least,* he thought, *those big ears will give me something to hold on to.*

With a lunge, Joe grabbed a leg, but the pig jerked loose. Joe pursued it and grabbed it again. This time he grasped the other leg.

Puffing heavily, Joe thought, *now to get it into the pen.*

Too Tall had a pig as well and was trying to wheelbarrow him toward *his* team's pen.

Joe grinned to himself. *That's not the way!*

Suddenly, Brittany Adkins bumped into Joe, causing both of them to fall into the mud. Brittany's pig stepped on Joe's leg. He lost his grip and the red pig scampered away.

"Sorry," Brittany shrugged, staggering off after another pig.

Joe wiped his muddy hands on his jeans as a boy went by dragging a black and white pig. Looking over the arena, Joe located Cuda. Arms outspread, Cuda looked as though he were trying to defend against a fast guard in basketball. Instead, it was a long, white gilt with a pink snout. As the pig bolted, Cuda reached out and grabbed its ear. Putting his arms around its middle, Cuda and the pig looked as though they were in a wrestling match. Finally, Cuda managed to pick it up.

I don't believe it! He's going to try and carry it to the pen, Joe thought. *He'll never make it.*

A black and white spotted pig, trailed by a red-headed

Crossover Dribble

boy, came right at Joe. *Sorry,* thought Joe, *all's fair in love and pig catching.* Joe put his legs together just as the pig ran into him. The sandy pant legs helped Joe trap the pig between his knees.

Now what, Joe thought. *The pig's going the opposite way from the pen. If I move, the pig will get away. If I don't move, we'll lose.*

The pig struggled to get away. As it squirmed, it stuck its foot in Joe's sneaker, knocking the shoe off. Joe spun and grabbed the pig's back legs and began backing toward the pen. With each step the pig squealed and twisted to get away. Slowly, Joe and the pig made their way across the arena. A quick glance told Joe that Cuda was still attempting to carry his pig through the mud.

Okay, fella, just a few more steps and we'll get what we both want. You'll be free and in the pen, and I'll be finished and in first place for the event. Just a few more steps...

Finally Joe dragged the pig through the gate and into the sawdust-filled pen. Holding the pig with one hand, he pulled the gate closed with his free hand.

"Hurry, Cuda! Come on," Joe urged.

Clearly the porker was all Cuda could handle. It was one of the largest pigs in the group. Joe shouted to Cuda, "You're real close now. Just hang on!"

The pig's head flopped from side to side as it squealed in Cuda's ears. The mud was ankle deep and the pig was

PJ Farris

covered in a mixture of muck and cooking oil that made it ever so slippery to hold. Cuda was doing his best to bear-hug the pig but it looked as though they were slow dancing across the sloppy arena. Meanwhile, Too Tall was struggling with his pig while Nate had his pig already in the pen. The race was now between Cuda and Too Tall. Cuda's face was flushed, his breathing hard. Too Tall looked ready to drop at any moment. Still both boys held onto their pigs.

As they approached their respective pens, the crowd roared encouragement. Too Tall, like Joe, had found that dragging the pig was easier than trying to push it. Cuda hugged his pig as though it were a giant bag of money. Too Tall got to the pen first, tugging on the pig to pull it into the pen. Meanwhile, Cuda lifted his pig in an effort to drop it into the pen.

Bang! The gun went off. "And we have a winner, ladies and gentlemen! The $500 first-place prize for the Farm Hand Contest goes to," the microphone crackled, "Nate and Tim 'Too Tall' Thompson." The crowd cheered and applauded.

Crushed with disappointment, Joe held onto a post. Cuda leaned on the gate, both gasping for air.

"That was one heavy hog, Man!" Cuda stammered.

"We lost, Cuda," Joe said. "I'm sorry."

"It wasn't your fault, Joe," Cuda panted. "I'm the one who let the pig get the best of me."

Crossover Dribble

The announcer interrupted again. "Second place of two $100 gift certificates goes to Joe Perkins and Ezekiel Rodriguez." There were more cheers and applause.

"Hey, Man! At least we won something," Cuda remarked.

"Yeah, right," Joe muttered as he wiped off the mud from the sneaker another contestant had retrieved for him. "I guess a hundred dollars worth of oil filters and cattle feed is better than nuthin'."

"Not oil filters, Man. The gift certificates are from Cooper's Department Store," Cuda said. "New sneakers for basketball season, Joe!" Cuda's elbow nudged Joe's ribs.

The judge handed the gift certificates—in plastic bags—to Joe and Cuda. As Cuda turned to leave the arena, he stumbled. Reaching out, he grabbed the bunting on the railing pulling it along with him down into the mud. Joe laughed as Cuda used the colorful bunting to wipe the mud from his face.

Hoisting the gift certificate triumphantly over his head, Cuda said, "Say, Man! All that pig chasing and carrying has made me hungry. Let's go get something to eat."

Joe laughed. "Yeah. How 'bout some barbeque porkchops?"

Cuda swung his filthy arm over Joe's equally dirty shoulder. "That will be my true revenge, Man!" Laughing, they waded through the mud and out of the arena.

Chapter 15
Rats

On Monday after the fair had ended, Captain and Joe rounded up the hens to sell. Joe's mom decided she didn't have time to sell eggs and work two jobs. Captain muttered that he always knew the egg business was too much work for too little profit.

Cuda was off swimming with some friends. *Lucky stiff,* Joe thought, *but he's earned some time off.*

While his mom drove off to her new job, Captain and Joe did the chores before they loaded the chicken crates onto the pickup.

"Watch out, Captain! There's a rat!" Joe yelled. The brown rodent ran along the back wall of the henhouse as Joe seized the legs of the remaining hen.

"Get some rat poison from the barn and put it down those rat holes. Then wash up so we can leave," Captain said.

A box with packets of rat poison was on a shelf in the

Crossover Dribble

barn. Joe picked up a couple of packets and went back to the chicken house. Hurriedly, he tossed the bags of poison onto the floor. *I'll stuff the packets down the rat holes when I get back,* he thought, *and ran to the house to clean up.*

The drive to the sale barn was a long winding one. As they drove along, they snacked on cookies. Captain talked about the countryside, farms and livestock they passed.

The sale barn had once been an old school gym. Perhaps that was the reason why Joe never minded tagging along on sale days. Bleachers ran around three sides of a pen with the one remaining side having two large wooden gates, one to let the animals into the sale ring and the other to let them out. Captain and Joe unloaded their merchandise and then walked though the holding pen area. Joe patted the three-day-old calves that had just been taken away from their mothers. They'd need a lot of attention until they could be weaned from a bottle to eating feed on their own. He watched the feeder pigs root up the straw bedding in their pen as they fought. Spring lambs butted heads nearby.

Taking his place at the microphone, the auctioneer welcomed the crowd with a couple of jokes before starting the auction. Eggs sold first. Captain and Joe had brought twelve dozen eggs that sold for $2.25 a dozen.

Captain leaned over to Joe, "Well, that's gas money."

The smaller animals were next. The hens brought $4.00 each. *Not bad,* Joe thought. The feeder lambs and a few

PJ Farris

ewes were sold followed by some goats.

When the cows and calves began selling, the crowd's interest perked up. A black cow with a white face and her calf were brought in, both were fat but terrified of the unfamiliar surroundings. No one wanted to start the bidding so the auctioneer kept lowering the price. Finally the bidding started. When it was over Captain told Joe the buyer had got them cheap. The next cow and calf were brought in, identical to the first cow and calf. The bidding started off hot and heavy, ending with a flurry.

Confused, Joe asked, "Captain, that cow and her calf weren't better than the first ones, but the guy paid $75 more for them."

Captain lowered his voice and whispered, "Buyers' remorse, Joe. The fellas doing the bidding realized too late that the first cow and calf were a real bargain. They ran the price up on the second cow and calf because they'd missed out on the first."

Joe thought, *just like getting the ball stolen from you and then getting mad and fouling the player. Better to stay calm and keep your poise, like Coach said. Use your head.*

For the remainder of the auction Joe paid close attention. His grandfather was right, the next item sold for a higher price.

The feeder pigs sold for 70 to 82 cents a pound.

Far too rich for my blood, Joe thought.

Crossover Dribble

The last group of feeder pigs was brought in. Their tails had been chewed off by other pigs.

"We've got six pigs here. Nice looking pigs. They average 20 pounds so they're already off to a good start," the auctioneer said. "All of these pigs have had their tails chewed off. Now, folks, pigs are just like us. We've all had our rear ends chewed out once or twice." The crowd chuckled as the auctioneer went on. "These little fellows are fine otherwise, what'um I bid?"

Already the crowd was thinning out. People were picking up checks for items they had sold or paying for items that had purchased. Others were loading their merchandise onto trucks.

"Come on, folks, these are real nice pigs. They'll do well for you," coaxed the auctioneer.

"How about five dollars each? Would you give five? Five?"

Captain leaned over and whispered, "That's cheap."

Nodding, Joe's eyes followed the pigs around the ring.

"How about four? Four? Four?"

Slowly, Joe raised his hand and the ring man signaled acknowledgement.

"Now I've got four. Who'll give me four and a half? Four and a half? Four and a half?" Joe's palms began to sweat as he sat staring at the pigs, afraid to look at the crowd.

PJ Farris

"How about four and a quarter? Four and a quarter? Going once! Twice! Sold, to the boy in the Cubs hat."

Relief flooded over Joe. An old farmer in bib overalls turned and said, "Boy, you got the best deal of the day! Put a little blue iodine spray on their behinds and you'll make money."

Captain, too, was pleased with Joe's purchase. "He's right. You outfoxed some pretty savvy bidders. Those are good pigs."

Maybe farming is like basketball, Joe thought. *Timing is everything.*

Feeling smug about his wise purchase, Joe settled up with the cashier. The pigs were loaded into the empty chicken crates for the ride home. Even with buying the six pigs, Joe still has some money left over.

As they drove down the lane, Joe spotted Scottie lying under the maple tree. The dog slowly got to his feet and staggered out to the pickup. Joe could see his throat was swollen to the size of an orange.

"Scottie, what's wrong?" Joe bent over and patted him.

Captain looked at the dog. "Maybe he's got a chicken bone in his mouth. Pry it open and look."

Grasping Scottie's mouth, Joe pulled open the dog's jaws and looked down his throat. "I can't see anything," he said, "Maybe we should drain the stuff out. We could punch a hole in his neck with a penknife." Joe had seen his father

Crossover Dribble

puncture small holes in the hogs that had small lumps on them and let the puss drain out.

"Naw, this don't look too good. Let's unload these pigs and take Scottie to the vet. He'll fix him up."

Spreading straw for bedding, they placed the six newly purchased pigs in a pen in the barn. Joe sprayed iodine on each of their tails and gave them a mixture of feed and water. The pigs put their snouts in the slop and grunted their approval. He looked for Scottie but the dog didn't appear.

By the time the pigs were settled in, the lump on Scottie's throat had gotten bigger. Now he was gasping for air. Joe fought back tears as he picked up Scottie and placed him on the pickup's seat. Never had Joe seen Captain drive so fast.

When they reached the veterinarian's office, Captain held the door as Joe carried Scottie into the examining room.

"Well, what have we here?" Doc Yoder asked as he looked Scottie over with a critical eye. "Why, this dog's been eating rat poison!"

"Rat poison! Oh, no," Joe turned pale—then red. "Doc, it's all my fault. I put it out this morning to kill rats in the chicken house. I must not have closed the door all the way."

"That stuff's not to be fooled with. It's sweet so that rats will eat it, but so will anything else. Let's see what we can do for him."

Unable to raise his head, Scottie lay panting for breath

on the examining table. Doc delicately patted him before he injected a hypodermic needle. Then Doc shaved the hair from under Scottie's chin so he could tell when the swelling went down.

"The rat poison is causing his throat to swell from blood collecting in his neck. Eventually he'll be unable to get his breath. He'll die from suffocation if we can't help him."

"And I wanted to punch a hole in his neck to let the stuff drain out," Joe remarked.

"That would have killed him then and there," Doc said. "As it is he's a really sick dog."

"Are we too late?" Joe could barely hear his own question. His hands were trembling as he stroked the dog while Doc listened for Scottie's heartbeat. Scottie looked at Joe, his brown eyes filled with trust.

Doc pulled his stethoscope from his ears. "Well, Joe, I'll be honest with you. He's in pretty bad shape, but I've seen worse recover. Just hang around here for awhile and if the swelling starts to go down, he just might make it." Doc had Joe give Scottie a pan of water while he went in the house to have his wife bring the dog some chicken broth.

Joe wept shamelessly. *My carelessness may kill Scottie,* he thought. *God I love this dog! He works so hard and I pay too little attention to him. Scottie doesn't deserve this. How could I do such a stupid thing?*

Lifting his head slightly, Scottie licked the chicken broth

Crossover Dribble

from Joe's fingers. Doc checked on Scottie every hour. Captain had said he'd pick Joe up about five o'clock so they'd get the chores done.

Joe's head ached as thoughts raced through his brain like a roller coaster. Scottie lay motionless most of the afternoon. Softly, Joe stroked the dog's fur. "It'll be all right, fella. Just take it easy," Joe murmured. But he thought, *Scottie, you're in bad shape. You're a tough dog. Just hang in there...*

Promptly at five, Captain's dusty pickup pulled into the vet's driveway.

Doc said, "I'll check on Scottie through the night. They need you at home, Joe." Doc put his hand on Joe's shoulder, "Scottie's swelling is going down. If he makes it through the night, he'll be back chasing cows by the end of the week."

With a nod, Joe asked, "Okay if I call you about nine or so? Just to see how he's coming along?"

"Sure, Joe. Call anytime you like."

On the way back to the farm, Captain was silent. Joe didn't feel like talking about Scottie or chattering about anything for that matter. He looked out the pickup's window as tears filled his eyes.

When they arrived home, Joe did the evening chores while Captain filled the cattle tank with water, before coming in for supper. They were having ham sandwiches and potato salad, one of Captain's favorites. Joe was well aware that Captain blamed him for not being more cautious with

PJ Farris

the rat poison. At least Captain hadn't lit into him with a lecture. But Joe knew it was tearing Captain up to keep quiet. The kitchen was still during dinner as the family brooded over Scottie's fate.

The phone rang. Joe nearly toppled his chair over racing to answer it. It was his dad. He'd be released the following day and needed somebody to pick up his things. They'd be bringing him home in an ambulance.

Joe's mom scurried to get ready. Joe spent the evening channel surfing on TV. Waiting wasn't the easiest thing Joe had ever done. And now, knowing his dad would be coming home, it reminded him of the day of the wreck. When the dining room clock struck nine, Joe's fingers rapidly punched in the phone number. Mrs. Yoder answered.

"It's Joe Perkins. Could you tell me how my dog is?"

"Let me ask Doc." The silence on the other end seemed like hours to Joe. Finally, Doc's wife was back on the line, "Scottie's better. Doc says it'll be morning before we'll know for certain if he'll make it. Why don't you call back then?"

"Sure. Thanks."

Sleep was impossible for Joe as he tossed and turned, arranging and rearranging his pillow to no avail. He turned on the light and grabbed one of Coach's skill cards.

Crossover Dribble

Tip Rebounding

The key to rebounding is positioning. Height helps but you have to be in the right place and ready to retrieve the ball.

Block out your opponent so that you are between him and the basket.

Be ready to time your jump for the rebound.

Practice tipping the ball on your fingertips and hand. Sometimes you can tip the ball to a teammate or tip it to yourself. Tipping the ball can give a smaller player the advantage over a larger player.

Rebounding has a lot to do with physics. A shot with a low arc will bounce to the opposite side of the basket from where the shot was taken. A shot with a high arc will tend to bounce straight up on the rim, allowing an opportunity for a tip-in or a lay up.

Long shots, like those from the three-point range, will bounce off to the opposite side of the court.

Be prepared to react. Once you get a rebound, be ready to fire a pass downcourt for a breakaway lay up.

Pulling on a pair of baggy shorts, white socks and sneakers, Joe grabbed his basketball and went out to shoot baskets and practice rebounding in the moonlight. When his legs became too weary for shooting jump shots, he tipped the ball against the backboard.

Funny. Doing basketball drills is just like doing chores, Joe thought. *You've got to do them right so nothing gets messed up, and you have to do them over, and over, and over again.*

After midnight, Joe finally tired. He went into the house and took another shower. Exhausted, he fell into bed, but tossed and turned all through the night, waking once to get a drink of water and another time to go to the bathroom.

At six o'clock, Joe was up. He nibbled at his breakfast before calling to check on Scottie.

Doc answered the phone. "Yes, Scottie's drinking water and urinating, both good signs. I'll keep him here a while longer, Joe."

"Sure." His voice sounded mixed with relief and worry.

Chapter 16
Recovery

The yard needed attention so Joe ran the mower over it before hurriedly hoeing the tomatoes and sweet corn in the garden and pulling weeds out of the onions. These were things Joe didn't care much about but he knew his Dad would. The garden was usually his mom's pride and joy. This year's didn't look like much, but at least you could see the vegetables. The flowerbed, however, was more weeds than blossoms.

Butterflies filled Joe's stomach as Captain's old pickup pulled into the lane followed by the ambulance. Joe leaned on the telephone pole and watched as an attendant opened the door. Joe could see his dad and was pleased to see him, a smile on his face. A big hand reached for Joe's.

"Feels good to be home, Joe!"

"Good to have you home, Dad," Joe said softly.

As they eased the gurney out of the ambulance, his dad

strained to catch whatever view he could of the crops and the farm animals. Joe's mom had rented a hospital bed for the family room, placing it in front of the picture window to satisfy some of his dad's curiosity.

As his father slowly gazed over the fields and barnyard, Joe held his breath.

"Looks good, Captain! Looks real good!"

While medical attendants adjusted the bed, Joe poured large glasses of iced tea. Captain filled his son in on what work had been completed and what lay ahead. Cuda had been sent on an errand into town to pick up some bolts and spark plugs for the tractors.

Joe's dad asked, "Where's Scottie disappeared to? I thought he'd jump all over me."

Joe started to tell him, but Captain interrupted, "Scottie got into a little bit of rat poison, but Doc says he'll be fine. He's just going to keep him for a couple of days."

"Rat poison? How did that happen?" He gave Joe a piercing glance.

"It was an accident. Everything's fine now. Just wait 'til you see Sassy's calf. It's a dandy. And Joe taught it to lead." Captain winked at Joe and jerked his head toward the door. Thankful, Joe headed out to fetch Sassy's calf.

After seeing how well the heifer calf led, and that Sassy was fine except for the scar where the vet stuck her with a knife, Joe's father signaled a thumbs up from his bed.

Crossover Dribble

Relieved, Joe returned the calf to Sassy and did the evening chores.

By the time Joe's mom arrived home, Joe had started grilling the cheeseburgers. Joe's dad had fallen asleep, and Captain had seated himself in the recliner with a magazine. The phone rang. With two great strides, Joe answered it before it could ring a second time.

"Hello, this is Doc Yoder. Your dog is doing okay. You can pick him up in the morning."

"Thanks, Doc," Joe said with relief. "That's great news."

The day's events kept flowing through Joe's mind as he tried to sleep that night. The sight of the ambulance coming down the lane, the joy on his dad's face when he saw Sassy's calf, and the call from Doc. Joe flipped his pillow to the cool side and turned over for what seemed like the hundredth time before finally dozing off.

By six o'clock the next morning, Joe was dressed. But by the time he reached the kitchen, his dad was already awake. Like most farmers, Joe's dad had a lifelong habit of rising early.

"What have you got planned for today?" he asked. "You going to mow the waterways or sweep out the bins?"

Captain was right, Joe thought. *Having Dad in the hospital did have its advantages.*

PJ Farris

In the excitement the day before, Joe hadn't noticed how pale his father's skin was. Years of farming had weathered and darkened his skin but it had lost much of its color in the hospital, and he hadn't noticed the tinge of gray in his dad's hair being there before the accident.

Joe poured orange juice while his mom fixed eggs and bacon. "Thanks, Joe. How about buttering the toast?"

Well, Joe thought as he spread the margarine, *Coach says the best defense is a good offense. Here goes nothing.*

"What's on your mind, Dad?"

His dad cleared his throat. "Well, I thought I'd check on the livestock that I can see from this here window. Any that don't look up to par, we'll sell."

Joe understood. *The bills keep on coming,* he thought.

After Captain arrived, the four of them ate breakfast. His mom left for work. Captain washed the dishes and left to pick up Scottie while Joe took care of the livestock and Mack took a nap.

As Joe did the chores he made mental notes about the livestock, trying to remember which animals might be ready to sell and which ones didn't seem to be putting on much weight. The fattening hogs were pretty easy. He and Captain had already taken three loads to market. The fat calves were more difficult for him to gauge. His dad would have an opinion on them.

Captain arrived with Scottie sitting on the seat next to

Crossover Dribble

him in the pickup. Except for the shaved neck, Scottie appeared to be good as new. As soon as Captain opened the door, Scottie jumped out and trotted over to Joe.

"Good boy, Scottie!" Scottie wagged his tail, licking Joe's hands and face. "Looks like Doc gave you a buzz cut on your neck."

Scottie let out a low "Oooowwww!"

"Good to see you, too, fella," Joe's eyes watered as he bent over to hug his dog.

"Doc said to keep him quiet a couple of days, but I don't think he'll be happy doing nothing. I suspect he can keep Mack occupied by babysitting with him, and vice versa." Captain said. "That'll keep both of them out of trouble."

"Yeah," Joe agreed.

They took Scottie inside the house. Joe's dad patted the dog's head as he gave Joe a scornful look. "Pretty dumb, letting the dog get poisoned like that," Joe's dad said sternly.

"Doc said he'll be as good as new," Captain interjected.

"Dad said you forgot to shut the chicken house door."

Joe felt his ears redden as he petted Scottie.

Captain changed the subject. "Have you decided what to do about the feeder steers?"

"Well, what do they look like?"

Captain sat down in an easy chair and talked about which calves looked ready for market and what price they might bring.

PJ Farris

Joe had mixed feelings as he listened to their conversation. After caring for the calves for so long, they were almost pets. He knew each one's habits. The calf that was always the first to race to the feeder to eat, the one that would linger at the feeder long after it was empty, the stubborn one that tried to stare down Scottie, and the fat one that delighted in knocking the feed bucket out of your hands.

Captain talked about Joe's pigs. "They look real good. Joe drove a hard bargain."

"And I only paid four dollars a piece," Joe interrupted.

"Yeah," Captain spoke up, "he's a pretty good bidder."

Joe's dad nodded, "Pigs that size will bring thirty dollars a piece in another week or so."

Joe beamed. His heart had not warmed to these six pigs since he had bought them the day Scottie nearly died.

"Well, call the trucker to come and get the fat calves in the morning. Always a good cattle market on Thursdays."

Captain and Joe went into the kitchen—out of earshot. "I think he's surprised we've done so well, Joe. He told me he couldn't believe the crops looked so good and the livestock are so fat and happy. I think he thought there'd be cocklebur weeds growing six feet tall in the cornfield and the cows so thin you could see their ribs. You're turning into a terrific farmer, Slats. Almost as good as me." With that, Captain tugged on the bill of Joe's baseball cap.

Joe was dismayed. *I don't want to be a farmer. Not at all.*

Chapter 17
Hoop Time

"Hola! Man, that alarm clock forgot to wake me up this morning," Cuda explained as he arrived late one morning a few weeks later.

Arriving a few minutes late had become a habit, but Cuda developed a standard line for Captain and Joe. "Mama, she just couldn't get me awake, Man. I was dreamin' a good dream. I had to finish it."

I wish I had your carefree attitude, able to take things easy. No problems, no worries, Joe thought. *Whenever I oversleep, I get jerked awake—pronto! Even oversleeping ten minutes is big time trouble for me.*

Now that the planting season was finished, Cuda and Captain spent rainy days working on maintenance of the tractors and other machinery while Joe power-washed everything with wheels and filled up fluid tanks—gas, diesel, windshield washing liquid. Bolts were tightened and

PJ Farris

oiled under Captain's orders. Cuda specialized in changing the oil and filters in all three tractors, Captain's pickup, and Joe's mom's car. He also checked the air in the tires. Dry weather days were devoted to scraping paint off buildings and sprucing them up with a new coat of paint and keeping up with mowing the lawn and waterways in the fields.

Having Cuda around meant Joe could still work on hoops. Despite how long the days were, they typically ended with Joe playing one-on-one with Cuda, with Scottie curled up under the maple tree as the only fan in the stands. Joe's confidence increased as he became an accurate shooter from several different spots, despite Cuda's excellent defense.

"Hey, Man, that was a three-pointer!" Cuda yelled.

"Yeah!" Joe grinned, "How about that!"

With the toe of his sneaker, Cuda drew a line around the perimeter. "Any shot beyond this line is a three-pointer. This is downtown, Man."

"Sure, Cuda," Joe said. "But fair warning, I'm planning to shoot out the lights downtown."

"Just try it and I'll be in your face every time!"

Dribbling to his left, Cuda crossed over and continued dribbling. Unexpectedly he whipped the ball between his legs and drove to the basket for a lay up.

"Play some D! That was too easy!" Cuda flashed a big smile as he took a bow.

Joe shouted, "My turn." Earlier trash talking needed

Crossover Dribble

results—and pronto.

Backing down with his dribble, Joe watched Cuda out of the corner of his eye, though Cuda was over him like a net over fish. Then Joe raced outside for a quick trey. Swish!

"I put a hand in your face and you still sink the shot. Have pity on me, Man." Cuda whimpered.

Captain watched from the porch swing. "Hey, fellas, you two are getting so neither of you miss a shot. It's 'Deadeye' Joe Perkins and 'Clutch Shot' Cuda."

The boys waved off his remarks and began to work on their drills, passing and moving the ball.

"These drills are a whole lot more difficult to do on gravel than in the gym," Cuda grumbled.

"You can't get a true dribble on gravel," Joe agreed.

"Still, practice is practice," Cuda said. "We can make do, Joe. Come fall, I'll be the number one point guard this side of the Ohio and you'll be a starter on the eighth-grade team. Yeah, Man!"

"I hope so, Cuda. Coach says to work to get better. And we've worked ourselves to a frazzle."

"Yeah. We're both lucky to have had Coach teaching us the fundamentals. A lot of players never get the basics."

"I know," Joe said, bouncing the ball between his legs.

"Yeah, Man. You can tell it when we play the other teams. A lot of those players don't know nothing about shooting form or positioning for defense. Even their passing game is lousy." Cuda tossed a pebble. "You know, Coach is probably the best coach around."

"We're pretty lucky. But if we don't get back to work, Dad and Captain will have our hides *and* our fundamentals." Joe grinned and headed for the barn.

Whenever Joe and Cuda played basketball, his dad watched from the living-room window, arms crossed over his chest, face frozen. At first, Joe was intimidated. His dad didn't berate him for playing, but Joe always felt guilty about not doing something more important. Finally, he decided the only thing he could do was to show his dad he would practice harder and work harder, as well.

What Joe's dad couldn't do in manual labor, he made up for in giving orders—telling them what to do, "Better move the cows to new pasture." Or, "It's about time to wean those pigs." Or "You need to wash and wax the tractors and car. I don't want them to rust out."

Far too often Joe's dad assigned more work than Joe, Cuda, and Captain, together, could accomplish. Then he'd become upset when they didn't get it all finished.

"You fellas are going to have to get more work done or we won't be ready in time for harvest," he'd tell them.

"We'll be ready with plenty of time to spare. You just keep your shirt on," Captain replied.

Joe's dad grunted, "Humph."

He fusses and fumes at us, Joe thought, *each time some-*

Crossover Dribble

thing isn't completed when he thinks it should be.

Day after day, when Joe and Cuda played ball in the driveway, Joe's dad watched moodily from his window. Captain spent less time watching the boys and more time trying to distract Mack.

Once when Joe and Cuda came in the house to get a drink of water after a torrid game of one-on-one, his dad called out, "Come here, Joe."

"Yeah, Dad. Can I get you something?"

"Naw, I'm fine. I'd sure like to see you work as hard taking care of the livestock as you do playing basketball."

"The livestock's fine, Dad."

"Yeah, but a little less time playing basketball and more time paying attention to them will make them even better off."

Joe didn't back down. "I get your drift, Dad. But believe me, everything's fine or Captain would have boxed my ears."

"I'm telling you to see that the livestock gets first priority. Hear me?"

Chapter 18
Mack's Story

Haying season was accompanied by hot, humid weather. Hay dust made Joe sneeze and gave him a headache. Snot and chaff blew out of his nose like stringy, dirty water. Bucking 60 to 70-pound bales up on a wagon all day long wasn't exactly pleasurable work. By the end of the day he was filthy from the dust and aching from the weight of the bales.

This hot, dusty work didn't seem to bother Cuda. While Joe was clad in a white T-shirt, Cuda stripped off his shirt, seemingly indifferent to the scratches of the hay stems.

"Cuda, how does a lazy dude like you get so many muscles?" Joe teased as they waited for Captain to arrive with the baler.

"Man, I'm not lazy. I just like to sleep in, you know—to finish my dreams," Cuda said as he poked Joe in the ribs. "Hey, Man, don't talk about me! There's not much fat on you!"

Crossover Dribble

"I guess not." Joe's arms were tanned to a coffee color from being outdoors all summer. Even relaxed, he could see the strength in his muscles. No fat there either.

Joe swung off the hay wagon. "Captain's sure taking his time."

"Yeah, Man. He's been gone a long time."

"Maybe the tractor broke down."

"Yeah, maybe."

Joe tossed aside the foxtail stem he'd been chewing. Captain was always prompt. In the wintertime, folks down at the diner set their clock by his arrival every day for lunch. "Cuda, come on. Let's take Captain's pickup and go see what happened to him."

"Sure thing."

Cuda drove the mile to the other hayfield. The old John Deere tractor and baler were near the opposite side of the field, but there was no sign of Captain.

"Drive across the field," Joe scanned the field looking for Captain. "I don't see him, do you?"

"No," Cuda answered.

A wave of panic hit Joe. *This isn't like Captain not to be where he's supposed to be. Something must have gone wrong.*

"Maybe he broke down and went to call for help," Cuda suggested.

"Who'd he call? We're the only ones around." There was an edge in Joe's voice.

PJ Farris

"Well, Man, he isn't here," Cuda said.

Joe looked under the tractor and beneath the baler. No Captain to be seen.

"Here's his handkerchief!" Cuda yelled as he untied the red cloth bandana from the steering wheel. "There's a note inside."

Scrawled in pencil were the words, "Gone to Ida May's."

"Who the heck is Ida May?" asked Cuda.

"She's the lady who owns this property," Joe said. "She lives over there in that little white house." He pointed with his finger. "Let's go see what's up."

As Cuda pulled the truck to a halt, Joe jumped out and ran to the house. Standing on the porch and looking through the window, Joe could see Captain sitting at the kitchen table.

An elderly lady opened the screen door. "Your grandfather was wondering when you'd show up," she said.

"Thanks, Mrs. Miller," Joe said, turning to talk to Captain. "Are you okay?" Then he saw a streak of red on his grandfather's chin. His pulse began racing. "Captain, you're bleeding."

"Bleeding?" Captain wiped his chin with his hand and laughed. "Why, Joe, don't you know the difference between blood and strawberry jam? Ida May made me a batch of buttermilk biscuits."

"Would you boys want some?" she asked.

"No, thanks," Joe said.

Crossover Dribble

"Nonsense, nobody turns down my biscuits and homemade jam. You boys sit yourselves down." The old lady scurried off and returned with glasses of milk and plates.

Cuda wasted no time buttering the hot biscuits and smothering them with strawberry jam. "Man, these are great! Thank you, Mrs. Miller!"

"Why, thank *you*, young man," Ida May said. "Want some more?"

"Sure, you bet. These are terrific!" Cuda said, wiping his mouth.

Joe ate a biscuit and drank some milk. "What happened, Captain? Did the tractor break down?"

"Well, I'll tell you what happened," Captain said. "The tractor ran out of gas and I decided that I'm too blamed old to walk home. I knew Ida May would be up and about so I thought I'd wait here instead of out in the hot sun until you two yahoos showed up. And as you can see, it's a pleasant place to rest and wait a spell."

"I was glad to see your grandpa, Joe. As soon as I saw him coming, I knew he'd join me for a snack," she said. "There wasn't no use in him sitting out there baking in the field until you boys came along."

"I guess not," Joe mumbled.

"Joe was thinking something bad had happened," Cuda put in.

"Well, Slats, things like this happen," Captain said.

PJ Farris

"Even to wise old owls like me."

"It's my fault, Mr. Perkins," Cuda said. "I should of checked the gas tank."

"Cuda, the gas gauge was right under my nose. I reckon I could have looked at it. It's no big deal," Captain said as he got up from the chair. "Well, we'd best be getting along. Now that you've got these boys as full as ticks, I probably won't get any work out of them the rest of the day." Captain winked at Ida May.

The elderly woman chuckled and waved. "Anytime you boys get hungry for biscuits and jam, just drop by!"

Cuda nudged Joe, "I could drop by every day!"

"Guess I could, too," Joe grinned.

"Yeah, and you'd be as fat as one of those feeder hogs and just as apt at working," Captain chided as the boys laughed and thanked their hostess for her hospitality.

A couple of weeks later, Captain was busy supervising Joe as they built a new cattle gate for the barnyard. Lying in the shady grass nearby, Scottie was busy snapping at gnats buzzing around his head.

"I told Dad I'm going out for basketball," Joe said as he sawed a board in half.

"I expect your dad didn't jump for joy over that news," Captain said as he drilled a hole and waited for Joe to put the

Crossover Dribble

bolt through it.

"No, he was as mad as the time we had the flat tire on the truck when it was loaded with market hogs." Joe cringed, remembering that horrible experience.

"Doesn't surprise me none." Captain chuckled.

"It's no skin off his nose. I do my chores and get my homework done. I think he's blaming me for his accident—like it was my fault or something."

Captain looked Joe squarely in the eye. "No, Joe. Mack is focused on farming and he expects you to do likewise."

Joe was silent.

"Hand me those bolts."

"I don't see why my playing basketball is such a big deal? Of course you or Mom have to pick me up after practice and take me to the games. Just once I'd like to see Dad at a game. The other guys' dads come. Even Scooter's dad comes and he lives an hour away."

Captain handed a socket wrench to Joe, who began tightening nuts on the bolts.

"I don't get it. Why does he hate basketball so much?" Joe asked.

"Your dad doesn't hate basketball," Captain said. "He just doesn't want you to drown in it, that's all."

"Drown in it?" Joe was confused.

"Your dad thinks the only thing you want to do is play basketball."

PJ Farris

"Yeah, I guess so," Joe said. "That doesn't mean he needs to ride me so."

"Deep down your dad wants you to one day take over the farm."

"But Captain, I don't know if I want to farm." Joe picked up a board and handed it to him.

"You know that, and I know that, and your mom knows that, but I don't think it ever sank in with your dad." Captain put the board in place and turned to Joe. "Did you know that your dad was a decent ball player in his day—a starter on the team?"

Stunned, Joe rocked back on his heals and looked at Captain in astonishment. "Dad played basketball?"

"Yeah. He wasn't half bad. Had quick hands like you have and was a better than average guard. They had a player, though, who was *really* good. That kid devoted every spare minute to practicing basketball. Your dad was almost as bad. He wouldn't come in at night until he'd hit twenty-five straight free throws. Guess I didn't get much work out of your dad during the basketball season. Anyway, this kid was one of the best players in the whole state. He played tough defense and had a quick jump shot. Catch and release quicker than you can snap your fingers. Why, that kid could steal the ball and drive in for a lay up before the other player knew what had happened. And could he ever shoot! One of the best pure shooters around. Folks said he had a chance

Crossover Dribble

to be the state's Mr. Basketball. That's no small feat, Slats."

Dumbfounded, Joe nodded.

"We were playing in the sectionals and had a pretty good chance of maybe even going to the state finals."

"We had a chance of winning the state tournament?" Joe asked, amazed.

"Sure, with a bit of luck. Anyway, just before the end of the first half of the final game of the sectionals, our team's best player was fouled hard and shoved into your dad. Their knees hit. Mack's leg was bruised a bit, but the other kid's knee swelled up like a watermelon. We won the game and went on to the semi-state. The players from the other team saw that our best player was hobbling and tried to take advantage of it."

"What did they do?"

"You know the kind of stuff that goes on. They pushed him and roughed him up with hard fouls. Mack was playing a whale of a game. He had fifteen points. The game was tied when a shot went up. Our best player and Mack crashed the boards, Mack undercut him by accident and the guy came down hard on his hurt knee. The knee blew out. That finished him. He ended up having surgery on it two or three times."

Joe was immersed in his own thoughts.

Captain pointed to a wrench, "Hand me that, will ya, Slats? Thanks. Well, that's not the end of the story. We lost the game in overtime. 'Course folks around here thought

PJ Farris

we'd win the state tournament. That was nothing but a pipe dream." Captain leaned back and rested his hands on his knees. "They thought it was Mack's fault that we didn't win the state tournament. We had a good team but it takes a special team, a great team, and a lot of luck to win the state. Well, our best player had been offered a full-ride scholarship to play ball for a Big Ten school. But when he had knee surgery, they pulled his scholarship and gave it to another player. Some folks blamed your dad for that, too. Your dad felt bad about it and blamed himself. Worse than that, some of your dad's best friends turned on him. It started out just teasing him, but then it got vicious. They wouldn't let up on him. That hurt your dad real bad, cut to the bone, you know? Joe, basketball is the only sport in small towns like ours. People live for going to the games during the winter. Shoot! If someone isn't at the basketball game, you know they're sick or out of town. And when his buddies turned on him, that did it for Mack."

"But why did they turn on Dad like that?"

"People got delusions of grandeur, big-time glory seekers you know. They wanted to blame somebody and Mack became their scapegoat. It got so bad that when he went into the barbershop, some friends would mock him or get up and leave—all over an accident. After a few years they let up on him, but he carried a huge burden on his shoulders. That's why he doesn't go to ball games. Why he got so depressed

Crossover Dribble

your grandma and I thought he'd have a nervous breakdown. We even thought about selling the farm and moving elsewhere, but that would have been the wrong thing to do."

"It wasn't his fault. With time running out, you've got to crash the boards and hope for the tip in. That's what Coach tells us to do," Joe said, "and Coach knows basketball."

"No, no, it wasn't your dad's fault, but you couldn't convince him of that. And the fellows were real hard on him. You know, the guys who are bleacher jocks with their loud mouths."

"Some friends," Joe murmured.

Captain looked at Joe. "People are funny. I guess as you go through life, it's tough to find a real good friend who'll stick with you when things go bad. And if you do find a friend like that, you'd better thank your lucky stars."

"I guess you're right," Joe said.

Scottie crept up and put his head against Joe's leg. Without thinking, Joe began stroking the dog's fur.

"Did Dad get counseling or something?" Joe asked.

"Naw, we didn't have stuff like that back then. Mack couldn't forgive himself or those diehards. He moved on and threw himself into farm work just as he had basketball. When he bought this farm it was run down and dilapidated. Now it's one of the prettiest farms in the country because of his hard work. Lots of folks would give their eye teeth for one of your dad's cows. He's done all right as a farmer."

PJ Farris

Joe nodded. *Why didn't Dad tell me about playing basketball? Why the big secret?* Joe thought.

"Why didn't somebody tell me?"

Captain put his hand on Joe's shoulder. "Every family has something they don't talk about, and no one wants to tell a boy like you that his dad isn't perfect. Parents are just human. Accidents happen. Mistakes are made."

Confused, Joe said, "I suppose you're right. You said Dad never got over the accident in the basketball game. What ever happened to the good player?"

"He ended up at a small college and set all kinds of scoring records," Captain said.

"Too bad he didn't stay around here," Joe said.

Captain turned and squinted his eyes at Joe. "He did, Joe." Captain picked up the tools and headed for the shed leaving Joe bewildered.

Restless, Joe tossed and turned in his bed that night, wadding up his sheets in a twisted knot. *Why didn't Dad ever say anything?* Joe was baffled. *If basketball was such a big part of Dad's life why didn't he ever talk about it?*

Joe flipped over and put his hands under his head as he stared at the glimmer of moonlight peeking through the curtains waving gently in the evening breeze. *All along, I thought Dad was trying to punish me for something,* Joe

Crossover Dribble

thought. *Maybe I was the one who was wrong. Deep down, maybe Dad still blames himself for what happened to their star player. I've been the chump. Me putting basketball above everything, like it was more important than life itself.*

A basketball poster on his wall could faintly be made out. Joe looked at it and thought, *That guy's a multimillionaire and lives for basketball. In a couple of years he'll be washed up and finished as a player. In a few years, people won't even remember who he was or what he did. Then someone else will be in the headlines and making even more dough.*

One thing with farming, no one's a poster boy. Day in and day out there's always work to be done. But just like basketball, you have to practice every day, prepare for what's coming up, take no shortcuts, work together, give good effort—and when the opportunity arises, take it. Timing is everything.

Turning on his side, Joe stared at another picture, a small one of himself in his basketball uniform. Number 23.

"I'm definitely going to make the best of it," Joe whispered. "Absolutely the best of it."

Chapter 19
Mack Mellows

The next morning, Joe's dad leaned on his crutches and peered into the back of the pickup at the two feeder calves Joe had loaded. "Why'd you pick those two?"

"Well, they're finicky eaters," Joe said.

"But they might come out of it and start eating again." Joe caught an edge in his father's voice.

"Well, they volunteered to go up the ramp. Since they didn't fuss when we caught them up, I didn't think you'd mind much," Captain said as he grabbed the steering wheel and climbed into the truck.

"That's no reason to pick out the two best calves and send them to market," Joe's dad insisted.

"Dad, they're not even average for our herd," Joe said.

"They might improve," his dad replied stubbornly.

"Come on, Dad, a lousy free-throw shooter might improve too, but they have to stand at the line and practice."

Crossover Dribble

His dad shot him a look causing Joe to turn away.

Captain jumped in, "Joe's right. These calves are last to belly up to the feed bunk."

Joe's Dad shrugged. "Guess you're right. Players who can't hit their free throws cost you ballgames. These two won't ever be winners. They'll eat enough to get by and never get much bigger. Sell 'em."

Taken aback, Joe couldn't ever recall his dad bringing up basketball without giving him a dig.

"Joe, get a move on so we can go sell these calves to some sucker to improve his herd," Captain said with a laugh as he started the engine.

Joe's dad and Captain were in a talkative mood as they rode along.

"We couldn't have picked a nicer day," Captain said.

"We could've gotten a lot of work done if we'd stayed home. If Cuda showed up, we might have repaired those holes in the barn."

"Mack, you're going to wear yourself out thinking up all those things for me and the boys to do." Captain chuckled.

"There's so much to do before we start combining the crops."

"And it'll get done just like everything else has, in due time, Mack."

"Guess you're right. It's just that being cooped up all the time with nothing to do makes you think up jobs you wouldn't think of otherwise."

"Yeah, Dad. Won't you catch Captain's drift and give us some breathing room?" Joe asked.

"Well, maybe. You guys did so much work while I was in the hospital, I just thought now that you have a good boss to oversee you, more work would get done." He smiled at Joe. "You know, crank it up another notch."

Captain nudged Joe, "It's time we form a union. Better wages and vacation time and all that stuff."

"Yeah. Cuda's soaking up some rays until school starts. Lucky dog! And you're planning to work my tail off until the first day of school. Ol' Miss Humphries's social studies class will be a welcome relief." Dramatically, Joe put his forearm on his forehead. Captain responded with a finger in Joe's ribs.

"Okay, I'll back off," Mack said. "If Joe's looking forward to doing those gigantic research reports Humphries requires, then I must be pouring it on too much—but a little work never killed anybody."

"Shoot, Mack, you never dole out just a *little* work!" Captain snorted and winked at Joe.

Folks at the sale barn greeted Mack, expressing their pleasure at seeing his return to the auction and activity in general. When the calves brought premium prices, Captain

Crossover Dribble

said, "Can't grumble about those prices, huh Mack?"

Joe's dad beamed. "Naw, they brought a good price, but a good calf *should* bring a good price." Using a pencil stub, Mack wrote down the price in a small notebook and stuck it in his shirt pocket.

Captain said, "Guess you knew what you were talking about, Joe."

"That'll help some, won't it Dad?" Joe asked, ever aware of the bills they owed.

"A little," his dad said, "but things will get better come fall."

Joe nodded. *At least I hope so.*

Chapter 20
Joe, the Farmer?

On a Saturday before school started, Joe's mom took him shopping at the mall despite his protests.

"You can't wear last year's clothes. Those are all worn out," she said.

"Mom, no one cares about your clothes, not the guys anyway," Joe muttered.

"Maybe not," she said, "but you don't have a pair of jeans that fit or sneakers without holes in them."

So Joe relented and spent the morning trying on shirts and jeans and buying new socks and underwear. At the athletic shoe store in the mall, they ran into Michael and his mom.

"Long time, no see," Michael said.

"Yeah," Joe replied. "Been busy on the farm."

"How's your dad doing?"

"Not up to working yet but the doctor says he will be soon," Joe hesitated a moment. "Did you go to camp this

Crossover Dribble

year?" *Like we both planned*, he thought.

"Yeah! Camp was great! Lots of talent there, let me tell you. I had to play a kid from Chicago who kept blocking my shots. I ate leather for lunch all week! Could he ever jump!"

Joe winced. "Sounds great. Wish I could've been there. Gotta go now. See ya."

On the way home, they stopped for pizza.

"Joe, you got the mopes?" his mom asked.

"It's just that the guys all went to basketball camps at colleges or over at Jefferson High School. Now I don't know if I'll even make the team, let alone the starting five."

"Joe, at the beginning of summer, I didn't think we'd make it. We had a lot of obstacles to overcome, and now—well things have worked out. I've got a good paying job, Dad's home and recovering, and the crops look like a bumper yield. Even the livestock is doing fine. We've done all right, Joe."

"The crops do look good, don't they?" Joe brightened up.

"Yes, thanks to Captain and you."

"Cuda did his part," Joe added.

"Yes, we were lucky to have him."

Reaching for another slice of sausage pizza, Joe thought, *We made it through the tough stuff, now it's up to me to make the basketball team. As Captain always says—never say never.*

PJ Farris

When they arrived home, Joe's dad and Captain were mapping out a strategy for the fall harvest. Stretching out in the recliner, Joe poured over the latest issue of *Sports Illustrated*.

"Joe, Cuda, and you can drive the tractors and wagons back and forth to the grain bins and I'll drive the combine."

"Sure," said Captain as Mack checked his list, item by item.

"Basketball practice will be a problem though."

His dad's words piqued Joe's ears. He held his breath and didn't move. He knew he shouldn't eavesdrop, but...

Mack leaned back. "That means we won't get any help at all after school during basketball season since Cuda'll be practicing every night."

Crestfallen, Joe buried his head in the magazine.

"What about Joe?" Captain asked.

"He'll have enough to do taking care of the livestock and doing his homework."

"But he wants to play ball this year, you know," Captain defended.

That a way! Joe thought, *Good ol' Captain never backs away from anything. Now it's right in Dad's lap.*

"Yeah, he told me." Mack tapped his pencil on the pad of paper.

Joe held his breath.

The wheels squeaked on the chair as his dad pushed

Crossover Dribble

away from his desk. "Well, I guess you could pick him up after practice. We'll probably need to take a break by then, anyway, for supper and the like. Joe can still drive a tractor on weekends for us."

His dad looked into the family room at Joe. "You're a good farm hand, Joe. We can't get along without you. Maybe you'll turn out to be a darned good farmer after all."

Joe's eyes remained glued to the magazine. "Dad, I don't like machinery," he said, deliberately picking his words. "I don't know if I'm cut out to be a farmer. I just don't know."

"Come on, Joe," his dad coaxed.

"Dad, I just have to make up my own mind," Joe's words were firm. "I can't be what you want me to be." Joe got up and headed for the door. Turning to look his father in the eye, he said, "I've got to decide for myself." Then he headed out to the barnyard.

"Joe!" his dad called out as the screen door slammed shut.

Chapter 21
All Out Effort

The end of August rolled around and Joe found school was a welcome relief. Lunchtime pick-up games with his buddies were refreshing. Even Miss Humphries' dreaded reports weren't as bad as rumors made them out to be. In fact, he found her history class to be interesting, and her dry sense of humor reminded him of Captain's wry jokes.

The weeks flew by until the big day finally arrived—the day coach made the cuts for the basketball team and selected the starting five. After two weeks of practice, Joe felt good about his chances. He had gotten up at 5:30 to get the chores finished in time to eat breakfast and catch the bus to the middle school. He'd dressed in Levi's, a Bulls T-shirt for luck, and had taken along the high-top sneakers he'd won courtesy of the Farm Hand Contest and Cuda's last ditch effort with that big pig. All through the day, Joe waffled between being eager to get to practice and dreading the bad

Crossover Dribble

news that it might bring.

Decked out in a tight-fitting black T-shirt and sunglasses, Cuda passed the yellow school bus in his recently purchased, used, shiny red Camaro which had replaced his old Harley. Honking his horn, Cuda gave a big thumbs up to Joe who was sitting in the back seat.

Good Ol' Cuda, Joe thought. *He knows what I'm up against. At least he's pulling for me.*

Joe's mind was racing. *The guys have spent all summer working on their skills and shooting. I've held my own during practice, but are they better than me? My defense is good, but what about my shooting? Will Coach notice? And if he does, will it make a difference?*

After school, Joe's stomach was filled with butterflies as he headed to the locker room. Nervously, he laced and relaced his sneakers. By the time Joe got to the court, Coach was coming out of his office with a clipboard in his hand.

This is it, Joe sighed, *time to suck it up and show my stuff.* Checking to see if the knots were secure on his new sneakers one last time, he glanced over at Coach's feet. Usually Coach wore warm-up pants but today he was wearing shorts. Above the ankle-high socks were two lines that looked like white railroad tracks. The scars ran from just below to slightly above Coach's right knee.

Joe's chin dropped in shock. Swallowing hard, he looked intently at Coach who was checking over some notes on the clipboard. Joe stared at the Coach's scars.

No wonder no one could beat Coach at a game of horse or in a free-throw contest, Joe thought. *One of the best players in the state—the potential All-American, the town's former hero—was standing right in front of him.*

A whistle blew, interrupting Joe's thoughts. The players formed a circle around Coach.

"We'll scrimmage now." Coach ticked off the players on the red team and then the white squad.

Coach paused. Joe felt his face redden. "Something wrong, Joe?" Coach asked.

As thoughts whirled inside his head, all jumbled and confused, Joe stammered, "No, nothing's wrong, Coach."

"Now let's see who'll hang around for the season." Coach bounced the ball twice and tossed it up at center court.

Michael tipped the ball to Aaron who gobbled it up. A bounce pass to Joe at the key freed Michael. Joe dribbled once and whipped a no-look pass back to Michael who drove in for an easy lay up. Michael turned and pointed his index finger at Joe, "Owe you one."

"Nice pass, Joe!" Coach shouted.

Too Tall Thompson took the ball out and flicked a pass upcourt to Jim Bob, a heavyset forward. Jim Bob headed full speed toward Joe.

Here comes the charging foul, Joe thought. *Gut check time!*

Crossover Dribble

Shutting his eyes, Joe braced himself. Boom! Jim Bob pummeled over Joe. Both lay on the floor as Coach blew his whistle signaling a foul. Shaking his head and checking his jaw to see if it was broken, Joe got up and ran down the court. He grinned to himself. Jim Bob was nothing compared to getting hit by Sassy.

Meanwhile, Jim Bob's teammates helped him to their bench. Skinny Billy Myers came in as his sub.

Joe's team had the ball. A teammate passed it to Joe, who faked a drive, then pulled up and swished a three-pointer.

Yes, Joe thought, *Captain's famous triple threat!*

Too Tall's face was filled with anger. No one wanted to be shown up in front of the coach, not when the starting positions were at stake. Too Tall took the ball out and drove for the basket. Reaching in, Joe stripped the ball away, directing it across the floor to Aaron who ran the length of the court for another easy lay up.

"Just keep feeding us, Joe. We can shoot lay ups all day." Aaron grinned.

Jim Bob returned to play and whispered into Too Tall's ear. Jim Bob threw the ball to Too Tall who took the ball up for a shot over Joe. Timing his leap perfectly, Joe swatted the shot away. Jim Bob recovered the ball and fed it back to Too Tall who did a head fake. Joe didn't bite. Too Tall faked again and then went up for a shot. Joe jumped, getting a piece of the ball on its way up. Grabbing the partially blocked ball,

PJ Farris

Michael dribbled it upcourt. He passed off to Aaron, who stood at midcourt dribbling the ball. Aaron threw a pass over to Joe. Threading the needle with a bounce pass between two opposing players, Joe hit Michael perfectly as he dashed through the key. Two points on another lay up!

Too Tall tossed the ball the length of the court to a teammate who made an uncontested lay up.

"Sorry, fellas," Aaron said, "I didn't cover my man."

"Don't worry about it," Michael said, slapping Aaron on the rump. "I needed a minute to catch my breath, anyway."

Aaron threw the ball to Michael who brought it upcourt and flipped it back to Aaron. Aaron snapped a pass to Joe who dribbled with his left hand, crossed over his right, pulled up, and shot a 15-footer. The ball arched high in the air, hit the back of the rim and rolled off.

Jim Bob grabbed the rebound and gave it to Too Tall, who casually brought the ball upcourt. As Too Tall crossed the center line, Joe bolted toward the ball. With his right hand, he knocked it free. Racing downcourt, he picked up the ball, pulled up, and banked in a 10-foot jumper.

"All right fellas! Now we're going to play basketball—no holds barred!" Too Tall gritted his teeth and threw a hard pass to Scooter, their team's point guard and best ball handler. He dribbled the ball behind his back and between his legs. Joe watched Scooter's antics from the corner of his eye. As Scooter bounced the ball between his legs to Too Tall, Joe

Crossover Dribble

reached out and tipped it up to Aaron. Aaron led Michael on a downcourt pass for another lay up.

Too Tall grabbed Scooter's jersey and screamed in his face, "Cut that fancy dribbling stuff! Just get the ball to me!"

This time Scooter dribbled upcourt and dutifully passed off to Too Tall in the post. Joe got an elbow in the ribs from Too Tall as the bigger boy leaned into him. Outweighed by at least 40 pounds, Joe shoved Too Tall back. Momentarily, the bigger boy lost his balance. Then Too Tall gave Joe a hard push as he drove in for the basket. The ball hit the backboard and bounced off. Using his rump to get position for the rebound, Joe blocked out Too Tall. Grabbing the ball with both hands, he tossed a pass to Michael who swung up to Aaron. Aaron blew the lay up but Michael was there as garbage man. He rebounded, then flipped up a shot that fell through the net.

Too Tall pointed a finger at Joe. "Why you little pipsqueak! I'm going to mop the floor with you!"

Joe stood his ground and glared back at Too Tall. Coach ran and positioned himself between the two boys. The two players glared at each other.

"That's enough, fellas!" Coach shouted as he put a hand on each player's chest. He turned to Too Tall. "Can you imagine what's going to happen when we play Northview and their big monsters this year?"

Too Tall's angry, stoneface crushed into a slight smile.

PJ Farris

"We'll beat the living tar out of them, Coach!"

"And Joe, I know you've been keeping the farm going while your dad was hurt, but I didn't expect you to bulk up and turn into a dang Brahma bull! Last year a feather duster could have bowled you over and now it'd take a bulldozer to push you around. And with those lightning fast hands and that incredible crossover dribble, you're gonna surprise some teams." Coach turned to the rest of the players, "Hey, guys, looks like we've got the talent to have a good chance at winning the conference!"

The players let out a loud whoop as they scurried to the showers. When they came out, Joe knew Coach would have the team posted on the wall next to his office.

Convinced that he had proven himself a starter, Joe could barely wait to see the results. Sure he'd missed a couple of shots today, but he'd hustled at every practice. Would Coach agree? The rivets of hot water pelted his body to the rhythm of the churning in his gut.

Joe waited until everyone else had left the locker room, then he quietly made his way to Coach's office. The list with the team members was posted next to the door as he knew it would be. He read each of the names:

Scooter Barnes *
Aaron Conner *
Chase Dobson

Crossover Dribble

Jim Bob Ferguson *
Dave Gordon
Terrance Hawkins
Jim Lawrence
Mike Mathers
Joe Perkins
Michael Rich *
Terry Too Tall Thompson *
Eric Vanetti
Jeff Wheeler

There. It was done. He had made the team. The tenseness in his muscles relaxed as he went over the list again. He was on the team—yes—but there was no asterisk by his name. Despite all the hours with Cuda, all the practice shooting and dribbling, he had failed to crack the starting five.

As Joe lowered his head and turned to walk away, Coach called him back. "Hey, Joe, wait a sec! Why the long face?"

Joe's shoulders slumped. *Go ahead, Coach,* he thought. *Dump on me like everyone else does. I'm just a second stringer.* Joe shrugged his shoulders.

"You've really worked hard on your game, Joe. I'm impressed," Coach said. "You know you're gonna make one heck of a sixth man coming off the bench."

Instantly Joe stiffened with anger. His heart pounded in his head like a sledgehammer beating a steel post into the

PJ Farris

ground after a drought. He thought, *why am I only a second stringer? I'm better than that.*

Coach explained, "I'm going to play a more aggressive game from the get go. We'll have our sixth man come in a couple of minutes into the game to give us a lift. Truth is, I'd like to beat the other teams out of the gate, but we've got some guys who turn tail and give up if we fall a few points behind. Then the typical sixth man won't be enough. Might as well chalk up an L before we even reach halftime. I need someone who can adjust and give us a good effort."

Joe's mouth dropped open. "Me?"

"Absolutely. I know you'll get the job done."

"So you think I'm just as good a player as the starters?"

"No, I didn't say that," Coach remarked.

There, Joe thought, *let's get it out on the table.*

Coach went on. "Talent wise, you're about even with a couple of guys. Head wise, you're more into the game. I guess life comes at you kind of funny—like that crossover dribble you've picked up. You never know what to expect, but you have to take what you've been given and make something out of it. It takes some folks a long time to learn that. Some never do." Coach put his foot on the folding chair near the doorway and rested his clipboard on his scarred knee. "You're a team player, Joe, and you'll help this team win." Coach stood up and slapped Joe on the back. "We need your versatility."

Crossover Dribble

Joe rubbed his chin, still sore from the charging foul he had taken from Jim Bob. The events he'd endured came to mind—his dad's accident, Sassy's mischief, the terrible hailstorm, Scottie eating the poison, not getting to attend the university basketball camp. And then he remembered the corn he'd planted, the doubling of the bean crop, scrimmaging with Cuda, and the Farm Hand Contest. *Maybe winning isn't everything. Maybe being open to new ideas and giving your best effort are more important.*

Joe murmured, "Okay, Coach."

Coach smiled. "You can do it, Joe."

"Thanks, Coach," Joe said, "I'll do my best."

"I know you will, Joe. You always do."

"Guess I'd better get goin'." Joe shifted his book bag and turned to leave when he felt a hand on his shoulder. He turned around.

"I don't think you read the whole list," Coach said as he bent his head toward the wall. "Check it out."

Baffled, Joe twisted his head to take another look.

Scooter Barnes*
Aaron Conner*
Chase Dobson
Jim Bob Ferguson*
Dave Gordon
Terrance Hawkins

PJ Farris

Jim Lawrence
Mike Mathers
Joe Perkins
Michael Rich *
Too Tall Thompson*
Eric Vanetti
Jeff Wheeler

Team Co-Captains: Aaron Conner and Joe Perkins